School friends

ecrets, hopes and dreams...
School friends are for ever!

Collect the whole **School Friends** series:

Party at Silver Spires
Dancer at Silver Spires
Dreams at Silver Spires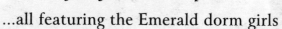
Magic at Silver Spires
Success at Silver Spires
Mystery at Silver Spires
...all featuring the Emerald dorm girls

First Term at Silver Spires
Drama at Silver Spires
Rivalry at Silver Spires
Princess at Silver Spires
 Secrets at Silver Spires
Star of Silver Spires
...all featuring the Amethyst dorm girls

Want to know more about **School Friends**?
Check out
www.silverspiresschool.co.uk

Mystery
at
Silver
Spires

Ann Bryant

USBORNE

For Ali Bradley and Jacqui Marriot
with love and all best wishes

First published in the UK in 2010 by Usborne Publishing Ltd.,
Usborne House, 83-85 Saffron Hill, London EC1N 8RT, England.
www.usborne.com

Cover illustration by Rui Ricardo for folioart.co.uk

The name Usborne and the devices ♀ 🏠 are Trade Marks of
Usborne Publishing Ltd.

A CIP catalogue record for this book is available from the British Library.

JFMAMJJASON /09 95200 ISBN 9780746098691
Printed in Reading, Berkshire, UK.

Chapter One

It was the middle of the night. I mean, the *very* middle of the night. Our dormitory was pitch black.

"Bryony, are you awake?" Izzy's trembling whisper came out of the darkness.

"Yes," I whispered back.

"Did you hear that noise?"

"I'm not sure...*something* must have woken me up..." I switched on my little night light. Then I looked round the other four beds in the dorm, but the rest of our friends were still fast asleep.

After a moment, when my eyes had adjusted

properly, I could see Izzy's pale frightened face. "Don't worry, Izzy. It's probably just one of those creaks you sometimes get in old buildings." But even as I was talking, I was thinking, *What rubbish*, because our boarding house, Forest Ash, is only about forty years old. I mean, that's not exactly ancient.

"Where do you think the noise came from?" Izzy whispered. "I couldn't tell."

I was about to say I wasn't sure when it came again – a soft bump. Izzy looked terrified and, though my heart was beating faster than usual, I felt sure there had to be an obvious explanation. "It could be a mouse or a bird," I said, trying not to sound too anxious. "After all we're on the top floor here. There's only the attic above us and nobody ever goes up there. I wouldn't even know how to get to it."

"But it didn't sound like a scratchy, scrabbly noise, did it, Bry?"

"Well no, but...let me go and have a look in the corridor. Maybe it wasn't coming from the attic at all. I'll be back in a sec."

I got out of bed, tiptoed across the room to the door and opened it as silently as possible, so as not to disturb the others. Matron's room was just along the landing from our dorm and I didn't want to give her a fright either. I looked right and then left in the gloom of the single landing light – it's always on in case anyone wants to go to the loo in the night. There was no sign of any of the staff or students, which might make Izzy even more alarmed. As I crept back into the dorm, closing the door behind me softly, and tiptoed over to Izzy's bed, I felt her fear lightly brushing me.

"I heard it again, Bry. Like someone treading really softly. I'm sure it's coming from above." Izzy fixed me with her frightened stare. "Do you think it's…a…a ghost?"

I frowned, then felt cross with myself for even considering it. "We would have known if there was a ghost at Forest Ash, Izzy. One of the older girls would definitely have said if the place was supposed to be haunted."

Izzy nodded slowly, then spoke in a shaky whisper. "Do you…believe in ghosts, Bryony?"

I'd never really been sure whether to believe in them or not, but now that Izzy was in such a state I decided it was better to say I didn't. I shook my head. "No."

She held my gaze. "*I* do. I stayed at my cousin's house one time and she told me the house was haunted. I definitely heard someone moving around that night and in the morning I checked and no one had got up for any reason. It really spooked me, and the thing is..." Izzy stopped and looked down for a moment.

"What?"

"You'll think it's silly."

"I won't."

"Well, the thing is, I got an e-mail from my cousin just today and she said they were selling the house because they'd all been frightened by noises in the night and her mum is convinced the place really is...haunted." She bit her lip and I wondered if she was going to cry, so I sat down next to her and took hold of her hand.

"Well, that's your cousin's house, not Forest Ash," I said firmly. It might have been because Izzy's eyes were big and round and full of fear, or because her face looked pale, but I knew I had to make her believe this definitely wasn't a ghost, or she'd spend the whole night wide awake and terrified. So I quickly told her something that my stepmum, Anna, had once said to make me feel better when I'd woken up one night and started worrying that I might get homesick when I came here to Silver Spires Boarding School.

"Izzy, things always seem worse at night-time.

In the morning we'll wonder what on earth we were worrying about. It's not a ghost. It'll probably turn out to be…a mouse…a heavy-footed one."

"You mean a rat!"

I could have kicked myself. Now she was sitting bolt upright in bed. "What if it finds its way into our dorm? I'd scream, Bry! I know I would!"

"No, it can't be a rat, because it would have to be really tiny to have got in through a little gap under the eaves or something like that. And there's definitely no way it could get in here. Honestly, Iz, don't worry. Try to get back to sleep."

I climbed back up the little ladder to my cabin bed and switched my night light back off, trying to take my own advice, but it wasn't easy because I was straining to listen out for the faintest sound. Even the familiar noise of my best friend, Emily, snoring very gently in the bed next to mine seemed like it was magnified a thousand times. At last all seemed quiet and I remember wondering whether Izzy was asleep, but I never found out which one of us fell asleep first, because the next thing I heard was the curtains being swished back and Emily's bright, bubbly voice saying, "Rise and shimmer folks!"

"*Shimmer?*" repeated Nicole in a sleepy voice. "What's that about?"

"I just thought I'd lower my expectations," said Emily. "I mean there's no way you can actually shine first thing in the morning, is there?" She grinned round at us all and I blinked back at her dozily. "Unless you're called Emily Dowd, of course!" she added.

And that was the moment when I remembered what had happened in the night and my eyes shot open and flew across to Izzy.

"Did you hear it any more?" I asked her.

Immediately she sat bolt upright. "No. Did you?"

"Hear what? When?" asked Emily, her head flicking from one to the other of us.

"What are you talking about?" asked Antonia, Nicole's best friend, as she sat up slowly and rubbed her eyes.

"Bryony and I heard a noise in the night," Izzy replied. "An actual noise. We didn't imagine it..." She was staring at Sasha, her own best friend, as though Sasha might not believe her. Then she looked up at the ceiling. "It came from up there!"

Immediately everyone looked up and if we hadn't been discussing such a serious subject, I would have felt like laughing.

"You can't *see* anything!" I said, rolling my eyes. "But we heard the noise quite a few times."

"It was probably just a bird," said Nicole. "They sometimes get into our roof at home."

"Or a mouse or a vole or something," said Emily, through a big yawn. "We get trillions of those on the farm." Then she went off to the bathroom and Nicole and Antonia followed. We could hear Antonia asking Nicole what a vole was. Antonia is Italian and, though her English is pretty much perfect now she's been at Silver Spires for almost three full terms, there are still some words she's never come across before.

As soon as the sound of their voices disappeared, Sasha and Izzy looked at each other. "Did you think it might be a...ghost?" Sasha asked quietly.

Izzy nodded. "It just didn't sound like an animal. It was too...soft and smooth."

Sasha's eyes widened. "Smooth like...gliding?"

I couldn't help feeling a tightness in my chest as though I needed to take a breath quickly. The common-sense part of me told me that there had to be some other explanation than ghosts. And anyway, I couldn't help going back to my first thought that we would have been told if Forest Ash was supposed to be haunted. No, it had to be an animal and I wouldn't let myself get carried away by any silly imaginings.

"Nicole and Emily are right. It'll just be a bird or a mouse or something," I said, getting up briskly. And the more I thought about it, the more certain I became, because I was remembering a time when we actually did have a mouse in our attic at home, right above Dad and Anna's room. My stepbrother, Robby, who's just a few months younger than me, agreed with me that there had to be at least six big mice – or even rats – making all that noise, and Dad and Anna got a pest controller in. But it turned out to be just one teeny little mouse. I could still see the man trying not to laugh at the looks on our faces when he showed us what he'd caught in the humane trap. "That's what all the fuss is about!" he'd said. "It's never as bad as it sounds, you know!"

I told Izzy the story and she managed the smallest of smiles at the end, then looked thoughtful. "All the same, we'd better report it, hadn't we, Bryony?"

I nodded slowly. "Yes…I suppose so."

As it happened, we forgot all about noises in the night as the day went on. The hot sun was shining out of a bright blue sky and the tall spires of the beautiful old main school building glittered like real silver. We strolled from lesson to lesson feeling as though we lived in a fairy tale. It was the most beautiful day we'd had in ages, because, even though it was June, there'd been quite a lot of rain and clouds for nearly a week. Every single student seemed over the moon about the sudden change.

Emily was probably the happiest of our little group of friends, because she'd started a gardening club last term and her vegetable plot at the back of the school kitchens looked amazing now that so much of what she'd planted was ready for picking. There are loads of girls in the club, but Emily is kind of in charge – even though she's only in Year Seven – because she seems to know more than anyone else about growing vegetables. She's been growing them on her parents' farm in Ireland since she was a little girl.

After lunch she insisted that we all go and spend a few minutes picking beans before afternoon lessons, but in the end we hardly picked any, because Emily insisted on giving us a centimetre-by-centimetre guided tour of every new shoot, pea and bean. The garden started off much smaller than it is now, but Stan, the old school gardener, just keeps expanding it. It's great, because we have so many more fresh vegetables for our meals now.

"Look at all these courgettes!" said Emily, her excitement quickly dissolving into a frown. "We've got to start picking them before they turn into marrows."

And, as if on cue, a bunch of Year Eights came through the gate and gasped at the sight of the garden.

"I swear everything's grown taller in the last two days!" said a girl called Isis.

"It probably has!" said Emily.

"Don't worry, when we've changed after school, we'll come back to work on it properly," Isis replied. "I just wanted to pinch a few pea pods. I love raw peas!"

Emily pretended to be cross. "So you're the phantom pea stealer!"

Phantom. It was only a word. Just a silly little word, but it shot me straight back to the noise in the night and when I looked at Izzy I saw her frown, then bite her lip, and I knew she was thinking back too.

Isis was grinning. "That's me!"

"Well don't nick any more or we'll have none left!" said Emily.

* * *

After school I went across to the garden with Emily to check she'd got enough helpers, then I joined the others, who were sunbathing – along with half the school – on the sloping lawns at the back of the Silver Spires main building,

"Isn't it bliss?" said Nicole, lying back with her shirt rolled up a little bit.

"I'd like it a little hotter," Antonia said, frowning.

"Hotter!" squeaked Sasha and Izzy together. "This is as hot as it gets in England, you know!"

Antonia laughed. "You'd think I'd be used to it by now, wouldn't you!"

That got me thinking back to when we first arrived here at Silver Spires last September, a bunch of Year Sevens, all brand new, with no idea what a boarding school would be like. I come from a big family – my dad, my stepmum Anna, three stepbrothers and a little half-brother – so you'd think I'd get along easily in a place that's buzzing with people all day. But actually I was quite homesick for two or three weeks, because I wasn't used to being surrounded by loads of girls and no boys at all. I'm quite a tomboy and, I know it sounds funny, but I don't talk as much as the rest of my friends. I just watch and listen. It's not that I'm shy or anything.

Just quieter than most people. Oh, and I set myself challenges too. I suppose that comes from having all these brothers continually daring me to do things. I can smile now, when I think about the fun we have in the holidays, because I'm completely settled at Silver Spires. In fact I totally love it. But when I first came here I felt really homesick whenever a picture of anyone in my family flitted into my mind.

All the Year Seven dorms are named after precious stones – ours is called Emerald. I remember how pleased Emily was to be in this particular dorm, because she comes from Ireland, which is sometimes called the Emerald Isle. It seemed the most obvious thing in the world for Emily and me to become best friends, since she was the only other person in the dorm who wasn't bothered about fashion or pop stars or TV or hairstyles. But, as you get to know people, you always find out that there's more to them than you first thought. And that's true of all my friends in Emerald. Nicole is a superbrain and got a scholarship to Silver Spires. Antonia is brilliant at languages. Izzy is the best ballet dancer I've ever seen, Sasha discovered in the first half of this term that she's got a real talent for rowing, and Emily knows more about growing things and farming than anyone of our age I've ever met. On top of all that, every one of my friends is a *real* friend. You just know you can rely on them to help you out if anything goes wrong.

As I like doing active things, like abseiling and rock climbing, the others all think I'm the brave one. It's not bravery, though, it's just that growing up with all those brothers meant I had to learn to hold my own, because I used to hate it when they teased me. Now, though, they never laugh at me, because they know I can do anything they can do. And here at Silver Spires, whenever I go off climbing or hiking, I always think about my brothers and feel happy inside when I imagine them high-fiving me the way they do at home.

It wasn't until Matron had come round at bedtime to check that we'd settled down and stopped talking, that I properly thought back to what had happened the night before. I wondered if I was the only one doing that.

These days it doesn't get dark till about ten o'clock so, even with the curtains drawn, it was still quite light. It was also very warm in the dorm and Emily had kicked off her duvet and was fast asleep. I couldn't tell if the others were actually sleeping but they were certainly very still. Even Izzy, which was amazing, because I hadn't thought she'd be able to forget the noises that had scared her so badly the night before. Maybe it was the heat of the day that seemed to have wrapped everything and everyone up and left us in a strange, sleepy daze. I certainly didn't think the noise would come again that night.

So when it *did* come, about five minutes later, my eyes flew open and my heart pounded. There was definitely something – or someone – moving around above our dorm. A muffled scuffle, then a smooth, soft tread, and a kind of rubbing. I told myself to calm down and remember the tiny mouse at home that had sounded like something so much bigger. I really worked hard on hanging on to this memory as I lay there, my ears straining for every sound. But in my heart I knew that, no matter how much I tried to convince myself that this was the same sound, really it was completely different. It just wasn't as scratchy.

"What's up, Bry?" Emily was propping herself up on her elbow, looking at me carefully. "Have you had a bad dream? Are you okay?"

I was glad it was Emily and not Izzy who'd woken up. I didn't have to try and be brave with

Ems. She's so down to earth, it was a comfort to have her near me. "It's that noise again. It's not like a mouse, Ems. Listen..."

We kept our eyes on each other and didn't move a muscle and after only a few seconds we both heard the noise. Emily's eyes widened, then narrowed in concentration.

"Actually," she said, thoughtfully, "I'm pretty sure it's a bird. Poor thing. I hope it's not stuck in there. We ought to tell Mrs. Pridham tomorrow."

Emily was right. And I guessed Mrs. Pridham would ask the caretaker to take a look. "I expect Mr. Monk will go up and release it," I said, nodding.

"Release what?" came Nicole's sleepy voice from across the dorm.

"We think it's a bird in the attic," I quickly told her.

The others didn't wake up fortunately and Emily flopped back down. "See you in the morning, Bry. It'll probably have gone by then, whatever it is... Night."

"Night," I replied in a whisper.

It seemed no time at all before Emily's deep breathing told me she was asleep. But I just lay there and kept listening. How could Emily be so sure it was a bird? Birds just don't sound like that. Wouldn't their claws make scratchy noises?

There wasn't a breath of air in the dorm and yet I found myself shivering as the darkness gathered.

Chapter Two

At breakfast the following morning I whispered to Emily not to tell Izzy about the noises in the night. "I don't want her to be scared again."

It was another hot, bright day and there was a lovely, happy atmosphere around Silver Spires. Everyone really likes Saturdays here because, once lessons are over at the end of the morning, you know you've got the rest of the weekend free from classrooms. Emily nearly always goes riding on Saturday afternoons and Sasha goes sculling. Sometimes there are organized activities, which are great, but at other times you really don't want to do much, and today felt like one of those days.

As soon as Emily and Sasha had gone, I went to e-mail Dad and Anna, then I joined the others, who were lying on the lawn. I usually love reading and I'd got a really good book out of the library, so I was looking forward to enjoying it in the sun. The other three were sunbathing and chatting as I tried to get into my book, but somehow I just couldn't concentrate. It wasn't their chatter that was breaking my concentration. It was my own thoughts. I kept remembering the noise we'd heard in the night, and thinking about what Emily had said. Perhaps she was right and it was just a bird?

In fact she probably *was* right, I just wished I knew for certain. I found myself reading the same page of my book over and over again, because every time I got to the bottom of it, I realized I hadn't taken in a single word. In the end I knew I had to do something, so I jumped up.

"What's up, Bry?" asked Nicole, squinting at me and trying to shield her eyes from the sun.

"I'm going for a walk."

"You're not going in the direction of Forest Ash, by any chance, are you?" asked Izzy, smiling at me pleadingly.

"Want me to get something for you, Iz?"

"Yes please, my ballet magazine. It's on my bed."

I didn't go straight to Forest Ash, because I'd decided to see if I could find Mr. Monk – even though he hardly ever seems to be around at weekends. It would be such a relief if he could somehow clear up the mystery. I knew Mrs. Pridham had gone away for the weekend, so I hadn't been able to talk to her, and I wasn't sure where to start looking for Mr. Monk.

In the end, I just wandered around, keeping my eyes open and hoping for the best. I've always enjoyed walking. It kind of helps me sort out the muddled mass of thoughts going on in my head. My friends say I'm the complete opposite of a chatterbox and that I never waste words, and I suppose that's true. It's because I'm so used to keeping my thoughts inside my head.

I think it started seven years ago, just after my mum died. I was only five, so my memory of that time is pretty muddled. I don't remember a point when Mum suddenly wasn't there. I just remember being surrounded by people all the time, and having tea parties and picnics and playing games and going to the shops. Everyone must have tried so hard to look after me. I've got one clear memory of playing in a room full of brightly coloured toys, spongy mats and squidgy tunnels and slides, and having such fun, and then sitting down with an enormous cake in front of me, while kind, smiling people talked to me. That was the only thing that spoiled the day for me – all the talking. I preferred having conversations inside my head. On my own. It was easier.

Now I'm older I realize that people were probably just trying to take my mind off the sadness of what had happened. But I must have been too young to take it in because, to tell the truth, I really can't remember feeling sad. I don't even have any recollection of Dad crying, and sometimes now I think how immensely brave and strong he must have been to shield me from his grief.

But it's odd how, when you're so young, everything gets mixed up and distorted, because the thing I *can* remember feeling sad about when I was little is our lovely grey cat, Lana, dying. I can clearly recall Dad burying her in our garden, then holding my hand tight as I whispered, "Bye bye, lovely Lana" over and over again, with a sadness that felt like a stone sitting in my stomach.

Apparently Lana died just after Mum. Dad was

upset too, as he'd had Lana ever since he'd known Mum, long before they'd got married or had me. They'd got her from a rescue centre when she was already quite elderly for a cat. So she just died naturally, of old age. It's strange, but every so often I get a really strong memory of sitting beside Mum on the sofa watching TV, leaning right into her, my head resting against her shoulder, while Lana sat on her lap very still, like a lovely, floppy old cushion. But I try not to dwell on that too much as it makes me so sad.

I clearly remember asking Dad if we could have another cat, and him saying, "We'll see. One day." But even though I've asked him loads of times since, he's always refused. I so wish he'd change his mind, because there's nothing I'd like more than to have a cat of my very own. In a strange way I think it might stop me feeling so sad when I think back to the Lana days.

I realized I'd drifted off in my head again – what was I supposed to be doing? Oh yes, looking for Mr. Monk. My footsteps had taken me towards the shrubberies at the side of the lane that runs from the big Silver Spires gates right up to the beautiful, grand main building that stands in the centre of the school grounds. Its spires remind me of sparklers throwing glitter into the sky whenever the sun shines. I jumped as a squirrel appeared from nowhere and went skittering up a tree right at the back of one of the shrubberies. There are lots of squirrels around the Silver Spires grounds. I used to be fascinated by their speed and nimbleness but I'm used to them now and, anyway, we're usually all so busy going about our own lives that we don't notice much wildlife activity.

I turned and walked back up the lane, then headed off towards the athletics field, passing the hazelnut tree outside Hazeldean. There are so many trees in the Silver Spires grounds – the weeping willow near Willowhaven, the line of beech trees curving round Beech House, and the tallest tree of all, the oak that towers over Oakley House. Elmhurst used to have an elm tree, but I've heard it got struck down by Dutch elm disease, and now they've got some lovely, shimmery silver birches instead. As for Forest Ash, we look out over a whole beautiful forest of ash trees just beyond the Silver Spires boundary.

I'm hopeless! I'd got completely distracted again from my search for Mr. Monk. But if he was here, he was bound to be working outside on such a lovely day, so perhaps I would find him at the athletics field. Or perhaps he'd be nearby at Pets' Place, where a few of the Year Sevens and Eights keep guinea pigs and rabbits that they've brought to school with them. Although the girls are responsible for their own pets, Mr. Monk sort of supervises the whole area.

None of the girls in my dorm have got any pets at Silver Spires, though I must admit, when I was homesick last September I did think it would have been comforting to have a furry friend to look after. My little half-brother, Adam, has two guinea pigs that live in the shed at home, and I often clean them out to help Anna, but I don't really feel as though they're mine. We joke that we share a cat called Fellini with the people who live next door to us, because he's always coming round to our house and Anna can't resist giving him titbits. He doesn't seem very grateful for them though, because once he's eaten he just wanders off and won't let anyone except Adam touch him. Adam scoops him up and leaves his back legs trailing, which doesn't seem to bother Fellini, strangely. I don't have anything like the same feelings for Fellini that I had for Lana. He's so different from her that he might as well be another species altogether.

I was deep in thought as I walked past the Pets' Place shed, which is about ten times bigger than the one we have at home. "Hi!" someone said, and I jumped round to see a Year Eight girl called Katy. She was in the middle of the big grassy area, where there are runs for the pets to roam around and graze, holding her rabbit. "Sorry, can you do me a favour...?"

"Yes, of course," I said.

She was standing beside a hutch that had a small run attached to it. "The catch seems to be stuck. It's kind of jammed and I can't undo it without putting Buddy down and if I put him down he'll scamper off..."

I quickly bent down and fiddled with the catch until I got it to move. Then I opened the door for Katy to put her rabbit inside.

"Thanks...it's Bryony, isn't it?"

I nodded. "It must be nice having a pet here."

She smiled. "Yeah... It really helped me with the homesickness, when I first came here, having something familiar with me that I could look after. Even before I joined it made the school seem less scary – you know, coming away to board and all that..." She grinned at me. "It stopped me panicking at the thought of what lay ahead in this big unknown place."

I nodded. "I can imagine..."

"Are you okay?" Katy suddenly asked.

"Yes. Fine. Just felt like walking. You haven't seen Mr. Monk around, have you?"

She shook her head. "I don't think he works at weekends." Then she smiled. "Thanks for your help, Bryony."

"That's all right."

It was quite a few minutes later when I looked at my watch and realized two things. One: Emily would be back soon. Two: I'd forgotten all about getting Izzy's magazine for her.

I made my way to Forest Ash and up to our dorm. The magazine was on Izzy's bed, but there was another one on her desk underneath and I wasn't sure which one she wanted. I was just peering at the date of the one on the bed when I stopped dead.

That sound again.

Only it wasn't the same. This time it seemed more like a gentle swishing. A mouse wouldn't make that sound. Neither would a bird...

"Bry! What are you up to?" Emily was standing in the doorway in her riding gear. "I was just going to get changed and come and find you. But you're here so—"

"Sssh! Listen…"

She rolled her eyes. "Not that 'ghost' again!"

"But…I don't get…what else could it be?"

We both stood quite still and only had to wait a few seconds before the exact same swishing sound came again. Emily and I held each other's gaze for ages, listening, as I waited to hear what she thought.

"So what are you doing inside anyway?" she said as soon as it stopped.

I couldn't believe it. She didn't seem bothered in the slightest. "Getting a magazine for Izzy. But what about the noise, Em!"

"It's just a bird. It's dragging its prey around." She started to get changed. "That's my guess anyway. Might be an owl. We had one in the loft of our hay barn for a while. Honestly, it sounded like someone was dragging a dead body around right over your head." She grinned as she pulled on a dark green top that went well with her mass of red hair and green eyes.

As Emily had been talking I'd felt myself relaxing, which meant I must have been tense without even realizing it. "Are you sure?" I double-checked.

She shrugged. "It'll be something like that, yes. Our owl was only there for a few days," she added. "Anyway, which magazine did Izzy want?" She

30

didn't wait for my answer, just picked them both up and made for the door.

But before she rushed off I wanted to see what she thought of an idea I'd just had. "Why don't we find out how you get up to the attic?"

She turned and rolled her eyes. "You're obsessed, Bry!" But then she broke into a grin. "Come on then!"

If you turn right outside our dorm you come to the big landing window. If you turn left you can walk quite a long way down the landing, past Matron's rooms, then turn a corner and walk even further. As it was such a hot day, and because it was the weekend, there was no one else about. We walked along the corridor and round the corner to the end, our eyes glued to the ceiling, looking for some kind of a hatch into the attic space. We already knew where all the various doors on this landing led to, so it had to be a hatch like the one at home. We've got a long stick with a hook on one end that undoes that hatch, and lets out a metal ladder that gradually unfolds into a staircase.

But there was no sign of anything like that here, which irritated me.

"There has to be a way to get up there," I said, frowning.

Emily shrugged. "Maybe it's just roof space. Not used for anything and no access to it. I mean all the doors lead to dorms or bathrooms, don't they?"

"Or the airing cupboard or Matron's room," I added.

"Or that other room. The cleaning room, isn't it?"

I nodded, but then frowned again. I'd never looked in there properly. "Let's just check."

We'd already passed it but we went back and Emily flung open the door dramatically. "See!"

It was a dingy room with a strong disinfectant-type smell and we were staring at a vacuum cleaner, buckets, cloths, detergent...and masses of other things. But no staircase.

Emily closed the door. "It reeks in there."

She was right.

"Come on, Bry. Let's get out in the fresh air. Race you downstairs!"

It was frustrating. There was nothing more I could do until I could speak to Mrs. Pridham at the end of the weekend. Perhaps Emily had been right to say I was obsessed. So now I was going to drop it.

I rushed off after her at top speed.

Chapter Three

That night we played a game after lights out, because none of us were tired. Saturday nights are good, because you know you can lie in bed on Sunday mornings and then have the whole day free. Well, sometimes you have work to catch up on, but apart from that it's a nice free day. We'd handed our phones in to Matron, which we have to do every night, and then we'd gone to bed and Sasha had suggested playing "Best and worst". So we'd waited for Matron to check we were all settled, and then waited a bit longer, because occasionally the member of staff on duty pops her head round the door a second time as a spot check. Actually, it's only Mrs. Pridham who does this and, as she was away that weekend, we knew we were pretty safe with Matron.

"Lights, camera, action!" said Emily, sitting up in bed and clicking on the switch, which lit up the little night light in the headboard of her bed.

Sasha and Izzy giggled as they followed suit, but Nicole and I stayed lying down and didn't bother with our lights. There was enough light in the dorm filtering its way through the curtains for my liking, and I wanted to feel comfortable, so I put my hands behind my head, and laced my fingers together.

The game consisted simply of taking turns to name a category, like *Best colour, worst colour*, or *Best moment ever, worst moment ever*, then we each took turns to tell the others our personal answers.

I far preferred the straightforward categories like colours or places you've visited, or girls' names. I found some of the other categories quite difficult because...well, I suppose it goes back to me being less chatty than my friends. There are some things I'd rather keep inside my head. Private, personal stuff. I've often been really surprised at how easily people discuss things that I'd never dream of talking about, and sometimes I feel a bit guilty, as though I'm not being fair to my friends – especially Emily

– by not sharing enough of my real self with them. It's true that Emily knows more about me than anyone else does – apart from Dad and Anna, of course – but I'm sure she still doesn't know as much about me as I know about her.

Tonight Nicole suggested the category *Scariest story you've ever heard*. I didn't mind that too much, because the stories could be made up or real. I planned to stick with a made-up one when it was my turn.

Antonia volunteered straight away to go first. "This is a true story," she began.

A tremor, or something in her voice, made me glance across at her and I saw that her eyes looked very round. Her face seemed paler than usual and somehow smaller too. It was framed by her mass of nearly black, shoulder-length curls, but her hair looked as though the ends were singed because of the eerie glow that her night light was casting over her.

"Aunt Angela – my mother's sister," she began, speaking as always with just a trace of an Italian accent, "used to live in a really ancient town in Italy that is supposed to be the most haunted place in the whole country. She moved there for her job and was to be sharing a flat with her friend, because it was before she got married. But the friend changed her mind at the last minute so Aunt Angela had to live on her own until she could get someone else to share with her."

I glanced at Izzy, because I wasn't so sure that a story about the most haunted place in Italy was such a great idea, but Izzy didn't look scared, just curious.

"The first time Aunt Angela saw the apartment she thought it was very old-fashioned and...what is that word...?"

"Quaint?" suggested Nicole.

"Yes, quaint!" said Antonia. "And sweet. It was winter when she moved in, so it felt cosy too. After a few days, my aunt started to feel rather pleased that her friend had not been able to share the apartment. It was so much fun having the whole place to herself. But then, one night, something happened to change her mind..."

Antonia paused and looked around the dorm to see how we were all taking her story. I looked around too, still feeling anxious about Izzy, but she didn't seem fazed – not yet anyway.

"So what happened?" Emily asked in a gabble.

"Well, when she came home from work she saw that a photo frame that had been on the top of her cupboard was now on the other side of the room.

And upstairs she found her toothbrush on the floor, and yet she had definitely left it in the glass."

"What, definitely?" asked Nicole. "I mean couldn't it have fallen out?"

"Well it *could* have done, but then she found that all the pictures in her bedroom were just a little bit tilted, and the book she was reading wasn't in its usual place."

"I still think it could all have been a coincidence," said Nicole. And I had to admit that was what I was thinking too.

Antonia closed her eyes and opened them again, with an air of mystery. "Maybe it was a coincidence," she continued, "but when Aunt Angela was lying in bed that night she heard a rattle that sounded just like chains, followed by some soft thuds like footsteps, and by this time she was terrified, being all alone."

"I would have phoned someone and got them to come round," said Sasha, shivering.

"Yes, then dived under the bedclothes," added Izzy shakily.

"Well, she did dive under the bedclothes," said Antonia, "only when she dared to look out after a couple of minutes of silence, she saw a woman in a long white dress standing right over her. Aunt Angela screamed the place down and the woman turned to a shadow, then disappeared altogether."

"And did she ever see the woman again or hear that anyone else living in that flat had seen her?" asked Emily amid gasps from Izzy and Sasha.

"No, because she moved out of the apartment one week later!" finished Antonia.

Izzy shuddered and snuggled down in her bed. "Was that the best or the worst scary story?" she asked in a small voice.

"I suppose it was both," said Antonia. "Or neither. Just the scariest."

"It was certainly that!" said Sasha quietly. "Let's not have any more. I'm already a bag of nerves!"

Nicole, who'd been lying down, sat up dramatically and folded her arms a bit huffily. "And now we've got to try and sleep!" she said. "Thanks very much, Antonia. Very helpful!"

Everyone laughed and I suggested that someone told a funny story or a joke. "Only not me, because I don't know any," I quickly added.

"What do birds say at Halloween?" Emily offered, through a yawn.

"I don't know, what do birds say at Halloween?" we chorused.

"Trick or tweet!"

Then Emily laughed her head off, which was much funnier than the actual joke as she'd got big-time gigglitis and her face always crinkles up so much when she's laughing that hard.

"I can tell you some more if you want," she went on, as soon as she was able to speak again.

"No, that'll keep us going just fine!" said Nicole, yawning as Emily and the others switched their lights off.

"Night," said Antonia. "Sorry about my story."

"S'okay," said Izzy softly.

"Night," someone else murmured.

"Bry!"

It was Emily whispering my name in the dark and I was a bit annoyed, because she'd woken me up from a lovely dream.

I looked over to her bed. "What?" I asked. Then I realized she was actually fast asleep and I must have just imagined she'd spoken. Or maybe I dreamed it. It was very confusing.

"Bry…"

"So you *are* awake?" I whispered.

"Only because you woke me," she said in a voice that was thick with sleep.

"But I thought you woke *me*!"

"Ssh! Listen!"

We both stayed completely quiet and from above us came the softest of footsteps.

"You still think it's a bird?" I asked Emily, my shoulders tensing slightly.

She paused before answering. "Something like that." Then, when I didn't reply, she went on, "Oh come on, Bry, you don't believe in ghosts and neither do I!"

I nodded. She was right. It was ridiculous to imagine even for a second that this could be a ghost. It was only Antonia's story that had freaked us a bit. "No, but..."

"But what...?"

"But I want to know what it is."

"How are you going to find out?"

"I don't know, but I will. Somehow."

On Sundays everything happens a bit later than it does on the other days of the week. We get up later, we eat breakfast later and most people spend ages simply chilling in their boarding houses. This Sunday was just as hot as the day before, so everyone was outside enjoying the sun. Emily was working in her garden and Sasha and Izzy had gone off for a sculling session at Pollington Water, which is a beautiful lake nearby. Nicole had persuaded Antonia to go for a swim, even though Antonia had complained that she'd freeze. She'd only agreed after Nicole had suggested they could warm themselves up in the sun on the lawn at the back of the main building afterwards.

So I had the perfect opportunity to double-check every single room on the top landing and try to find a way up to the attic. I really wanted to go into Matron's room, to see whether there was a staircase in there, by any chance, but I wasn't sure if I dared. It was a cheeky thing to do. Of course, I could simply tell her about the noises, but I knew Matron – she'd only laugh and say we had overactive imaginations.

I didn't realize, until I went round the corner of our landing, that the three Year Nines who share the room on the left after the airing cupboard were still in their dorm. In fact, it was as I was passing their door that it opened and out they came, all talking excitedly about something. They stopped when they saw me.

"Oh! Bryony! Hi! What are you doing round here?" asked Nadia.

"I was just…er…looking for Matron."

"I think she went outside. She said she was going to read her book round the side of Forest Ash in the shade somewhere."

"Oh, right, thanks." I turned to go back to Emerald until they'd disappeared, but Nadia called after me. "Hey, Bryony, you lot haven't heard any strange noises in the night, have you?"

I hesitated, but there was no reason not to tell the truth.

"Yes…like there's a bird or a mouse or something in the roof."

The Year Nines looked at each other and I saw Annie nudge Gemma subtly.

"Yes, it's probably just something like that."

I knew they were trying not to scare me. "Why, what did you think it was?"

"Depends whether you believe in ghosts," said Nadia.

I smiled at her. "No, I don't."

"Anyway, there's sure to be some obvious explanation," Annie said. "We're going to tell Mr. Monk tomorrow."

I went back to Emerald and stayed there until I was sure they'd gone out, then crept back out and walked along to the airing cupboard. It was more of a room than a cupboard, because you could walk right in. Along three walls were shelves with piles of towels and sheets and blankets and pillowcases, but there were no hatches or staircases anywhere, so I went on to look at the cleaning room again.

It didn't look any different to the way it had the day before, but I had to make sure I wasn't missing anything, so when I spotted a light switch I clicked it on, transforming the little room. Now I could clearly see all the brooms and buckets and cloths and detergents. And I could also see that, right at the back of the cupboard, going off to the left, was a staircase. I walked slowly towards it, holding my breath.

Was this how the princess in the story *Sleeping Beauty* felt on her fifteenth birthday when she started exploring parts of the palace she'd never seen before? There didn't seem to be another light switch anywhere, so I tiptoed cautiously up the steep, narrow stairs, my heartbeat starting to quicken as I wondered what I would find. Did ghosts walk around during the day? I snapped that thought out of my mind instantly, because it was ridiculous and I knew it. And anyway it was far too hot. In any ghost story I've ever read, the air is always cold.

My eyes widened as I climbed the last few stairs,

because I could see the whole loft. There was a huge water tank with loads of pipes everywhere, making a faint buzzing sound and the occasional clunk. I didn't mind those noises. They were almost comforting. The beams sloped diagonally, following the shape of the roof, and there was a mass of dirty yellowy insulation. On a cold day it would probably be really cosy up here, even though it was a big area and a lot of it was empty. Along one side, old paint cans, brushes and rolls of wallpaper were stored. And next to them, dusty boxes. Then there were some unusual things that had obviously been dumped here instead of being thrown away, like a tailor's dummy and a globe, an ironing board and a microwave, a computer printer and piles of old curtains.

A proper window had been built into the roof and it was very slightly open. Had that window been closed I think the heat would have been unbearable. I started exploring very cautiously because, although I don't hate mice, or even rats, if one scuttled out of the silent shadows and ran over my toes, I might be terrified. And what if a bird or a bat flew into my face? That would be totally scary too.

But I was here to investigate and that meant searching every nook and cranny, so I ought to get on with it before anyone discovered me. The thought of being discovered made me freeze. Had I closed the cleaning room door? I couldn't remember. In the excitement of finding the staircase I'd completely forgotten that I didn't actually have permission to be up here. I had to carry on, though, and complete my mission. My eyes were still wide, trying to take in absolutely every centimetre of floor and wall and beam and insulation, but as I got closer to the far end I realized gradually that it wasn't the end. It lead round a corner. So then my mouth felt dry as my mind conjured up images of scrabbling, flea-infested rats, or – the worst possible nightmare – a dead body.

Stop it, Bryony, I told myself fiercely. *There won't be anything...*

But what I heard next made my heart pound in my chest: Matron's voice, muffled, as though she was quite far away. "Bryony? Did you want me?" She must have been outside our dorm.

This was terrible. I was sure now that I hadn't closed the door to the cleaning room. What if she came up the stairs and found me here, breaking school rules? I had to go. Right now, so I didn't get in any trouble. I could pretend I'd spilled something in our dorm and was in the cleaning room looking for a cloth to wipe it up with.

Then something happened that made me stop in my tracks. I was about to turn to walk on shaky legs towards the stairs, when, out of the corner of my eye, I caught a flash of silver-grey streaking through the tiny gap of the open window and I gasped at the shock and the speed. What was it? Some kind of animal. But what?

My legs trembled a bit as I went down the stairs, and my ears strained to hear whether Matron was still nearby. But there wasn't a sound. The cleaning room was silent and still. I *had* left the door about a centimetre open, though, and I felt weak with relief that I hadn't been discovered. I poked my head out really slowly and looked right and left, but no one was there. I shut the door behind me and hurried along the corridor and into Emerald, where I flopped onto my bed and thought through all that had just happened.

What was that silver creature? Then something clicked inside my brain. It must have been a squirrel. Obviously! I smiled to myself. Why hadn't I thought of that before? It had simply climbed up the wall and through the window. I mean it couldn't have been anything else. Certainly not a rat. It was far too agile – it almost flew out of the window. And only a squirrel would be able to get down the side of the building without hurting itself. I tried to visualize the wall. Was there ivy or something growing up it? I couldn't remember. We didn't often go round that side. But squirrels don't even need ivy. They run up tall tree trunks without any trouble.

In no time at all I was downstairs, then out of the building, staring up at the side wall of Forest Ash. It was almost completely covered with some kind of climbing plant that had grown up a trellis. The plant stopped at the roof but the attic window was less than a metre above it. So now I felt sure that the mystery was solved. The squirrel must have scrambled up and down this wall, clinging to the plant and the trellis. Easy peasy! I couldn't wait to tell the others.

Chapter Four

After that Sunday the weekdays seemed lovely and peaceful and ghost-free. When I'd told the others about going up to the attic, they'd gasped and seemed a bit disapproving. "You might have got caught!" Nicole had said, making the others nod, wide-eyed. But then when I came to the bit about the squirrel, it was obvious they were relieved, especially Izzy. "Thank goodness for that, Bry!" she'd said. And she'd looked at me really gratefully.

I guessed the Year Nines must have reported the noises they'd heard to Mr. Monk, and he'd probably stopped the squirrel coming in. All I know is that none of us in Emerald heard anything more from the attic, night or day, and after a while I forgot about how fazed I'd been.

The following Friday was the introductory day for the new Year Sevens who would be coming to Silver Spires in September. Seeing them all around the place took me right back to my own introductory day. The main thing I remember was the feeling that I might not fit in because I wasn't somehow girlie enough. I didn't actually meet Emily that day; I didn't really meet anyone. It was as though I was there, but I wasn't a part of it. I just watched everything that was going on, and listened to other people talking and laughing and seeming excited.

"Don't forget to look out for a girl with really short dark reddy-brown hair," Sasha reminded us.

Her mum had phoned a few days before to say that a girl called Hannah Chadwick, who was the daughter of someone she worked with, would be coming on the introductory day. Sasha could remember Hannah from Year Four at primary, but then they'd lost touch, because Hannah and her family had moved a few miles away and Hannah had started at a different school.

"She was really nice actually," Sasha had told us. "Very shy, though."

"They look so young," said Izzy, when we'd just passed a group of girls quietly walking along with a member of staff.

"And...scared..." added Nicole. "Like *I* was." She did a dramatic shudder as though she wouldn't want to go back to those days.

"Me too," I said, to make her feel better.

Then the others all nodded in agreement. "Yes, same here."

"It didn't take long to get used to it, though, did it?" said Emily.

"That's the magic of Silver Spires!" said Antonia, her eyes sparkling.

That night I dreamed I was walking with Mum and she was carrying our old cat Lana in a baby sling. It was a weird dream but a happy one. Dad said that when I was a baby Mum had walked for miles with me on her front in a sling, so my dream was just a bit mixed up, that's all. I woke up with the clearest picture of Mum's face in my mind. She was very dark like me and had short hair like me, too, and didn't wear make-up. I remember her wearing jeans and T-shirts a lot. At least I think I'm remembering and not just thinking of the photos I've seen.

I smiled to myself in the dark, because I like the thought that there might be a gene that I've inherited from Mum that makes you love walking. Then my thoughts turned to all the new girls who'd been around during the day. We hadn't come across Hannah at all, and in the end we'd asked Mrs. Pridham if she was actually there. She'd told us that Hannah was ill and would have to come on her own another day. Poor thing, I thought, turning over and closing my eyes.

Then I froze, because I heard something from the attic. Only this time it wasn't footsteps, or scrabbling or rubbing or dragging – and it didn't sound anything like a squirrel! It was a cry. Like a baby. My hand shot to my mouth as though I'd made the sound myself. How could it be a baby? Unless it was... the ghost of a baby?

I don't know how I ever got myself back to sleep that night, but I must have done somehow. The next day when I woke up I felt so tired. I obviously looked it too, because Emily kept on asking me if I was all right.

In the end I told her what I'd heard. "But don't tell the others, whatever you do. They'd be terrified."

"But...a *baby*, Bry? Are you sure you didn't imagine it?"

I shook my head. "One hundred per cent. Something was crying up there, and I want to go back and find out what's going on, Ems. I can't stand mysteries."

"I'll come with you," she said straight away.

I nodded, feeling relieved. I was actually quite anxious about going on my own.

So we decided we'd go as soon as she got back from riding.

I've never known time pass as slowly as it did that Saturday. It was another beautiful hot day but I couldn't enjoy the sun, because my mind was on the attic and what we might find up there.

I met Emily from the minibus when she got back from riding. She didn't even bother to get changed. We just went straight along the third-floor landing to the cleaning room, and were relieved that there was no one around again. I wasn't so worried about getting caught this time, because I was careful to shut the door to the cleaning room behind us.

Emily was just as surprised as I'd been to see how big the attic was. "Do you think we'd be in trouble if anyone knew we were up here?" she said in a whisper, staring around.

I nodded.

"But we've never exactly been *told* it's out of bounds, have we?"

"No, but..."

Emily frowned, then pointed to the far end of the loft. "What's round there?"

"I'm not sure. That's where the squirrel came from though." I took a couple of steps towards it.

"You ought to be careful, Bry. I've heard squirrels can scratch and bite and really hurt you."

I didn't care. In fact I was still really hoping we'd see the squirrel. I couldn't forget that little cry though, and squirrels just don't cry. What else was I about to find? My mouth felt dry as I tiptoed forwards, centimetre by centimetre, with the quietest footsteps, while Emily hung back.

"Can you see anything, Bry?"

I only just heard her whisper from behind me as I turned the corner, and then I gasped but quickly stifled it. Sitting in front of me, upright and stiff, ears pricked, was a thin waif of a cat. It had a whitish streak running down its nose and dark eyes which met mine for a second, before it fled past me to the open window like a silver arrow. A cat, I couldn't believe it. So it wasn't a squirrel after all!

"A cat!" said Emily. "Phew!" She let out her breath. "Mystery solved! Let's go before we get caught."

I don't know why but I felt a stab of disappointment that Emily was taking it so casually. To me it was a shock. I'd never expected a cat. A cat was completely different from a squirrel. My mind was spinning. "Don't you wonder what it's doing up here? I mean, why does it keep coming back?"

Emily shrugged. "Cats get into the weirdest places."

"I suppose they do," I answered thoughtfully, remembering the first time we'd found Fellini sitting in a spare washing-up bowl we kept on top of the freezer. He looked so funny. But he obviously liked it there because he kept coming back.

I wanted to get back to talking about the cat we'd just found though. "It looked really thin, didn't it?"

"It's probably a stray," Emily said, turning to go. "Come on, Bry. Remember we're not supposed to be up here."

I bent down and touched the hollowed-out place where the cat had been sitting. It still felt warm and I was really sorry that I'd frightened it away twice now. "It must have been cosy on this pile of dust sheets, mustn't it?"

But Emily was heading for the stairs. "We'd better report it to Mrs. Pridham, Bry. Come on."

"No, let's not," I said, hurrying after her. "Mrs. P wouldn't want a stray cat at Forest Ash. She'd only get rid of it. Let's see it one more time, properly, before we tell her. Maybe we can help it."

A part of me felt completely detached from the rest of me. It was like I was listening to myself saying these things and wondering why. But the part that was actually saying them thought it was completely natural. Maybe my dream about Lana had affected me more than I'd thought it had. *Something* certainly had, because for some reason I really cared about the cat. I couldn't just dismiss it out of hand. It seemed important that we made sure it could manage all right, especially if it was a stray with no one to feed it, and nowhere to snuggle down at night.

"Where does it get its food, do you think, Ems?"

"Hunting mice and birds... And it probably goes further afield than Silver Spires. I guess it looks for scraps that people have thrown out with their rubbish..." Emily suddenly turned round to face me, a finger on her lips, to tell me we should stop talking now. Then just as I'd done before, she looked right and left before risking coming out of the cleaning room onto the landing.

I waited till we were in our dorm and Emily was getting changed out of her riding gear before I mentioned the cat again. "But don't you feel sorry for it, Ems?"

She shrugged but didn't answer my question and I guessed that any cats she might have come across on the farm were probably really independent, so she wouldn't have felt any attachment to them.

"Ems," I said carefully, "let's not tell the others just yet, otherwise they'll all want to go up and see it, and I don't want to frighten it away for good. Let's not tell...Mrs. Pridham either for now."

Emily put her arm round me. "You're so sweet, Bry," she said. "Don't worry, I won't mention it to anyone." Then she looked suddenly serious. "But even if it doesn't get frightened away for good, it'll only run away every time you go up there. I mean, you won't be able to have it as a pet or anything. It's wild, Bry."

I sighed as I realized that although I hadn't admitted it, even to myself, I really did wish I could look after it...and, yes, maybe even keep it.

"Come on, let's go and see what's happening in the garden, yeah?"

I followed her downstairs and out of Silver Spires, and as she chatted away about the hack she'd just been on through the woods, I couldn't help my mind drifting back to the cat. In a way it reminded me of Lana, only it was more silvery and miles thinner. It was nothing like Fellini. Fellini is black and white and stalks about grandly as though he owns the world. This cat seemed quite the opposite. Frightened and fleeting. I wished I could calm it down so it wouldn't run away all the time, poor thing.

I wanted to give it a name, but I couldn't think of anything original, so I decided to be totally unoriginal and name it after its colour. *Silver*. Yes, that would be fine, just until I came up with something better. And I made another decision too. Despite what Emily had said, I decided I would try and smuggle some food out from supper, and take it up to Silver as soon as possible. That might tempt him to stay, and make him a bit less wild and afraid too. But maybe I'd wait till the next day, because I wasn't sure if I could risk going up there twice in one day. Who knew what would happen if I got caught?

Waking up the next morning, Silver was the first thing to come into my mind. The previous evening, at supper, I'd managed to slip a piece of chicken into a tissue and put it in my pocket without anyone noticing. And while I'd been lying in bed I'd had the good idea of emptying a plastic tub that I usually keep my shower stuff in and filling it with water. Silver was probably really thirsty in this boiling weather. I couldn't wait to give him his little meal.

Walking back from a lovely big Sunday breakfast, it was obvious that today was going to be another hot day. Good, that meant a high chance of all the Forest Ash girls being outside soaking up the sun.

"I wish I didn't have to work when it's so beautiful," said Antonia, slowing down as though the very thought of studying made her feel tired.

"Let's get it over with right now," Nicole said decisively, "then we can do whatever we want for the rest of the day. What's everyone else doing?" she asked, looking directly at me for some reason.

"Er...not a lot..."

"Weeding," Emily announced with a firm nod of her head. "In fact I'm going to get my old trainers and cut-offs on right now." She broke into a jog, then called back over her shoulder, "Feel free to help me!"

"Sorry. Iz and I are going sculling again!" Sasha called back.

I couldn't help feeling pleased that at least two of them would be out of the way. I just hoped that Nicole and Antonia weren't planning on working in the dorm, because that would mean I wouldn't be able to go up and see Silver, as they'd hear my footsteps above them and get the shock of their lives.

"It's great that we can work outside now it's so hot," I said casually.

"Yes, but I can't concentrate outside," said Antonia with a sigh. "I get...distracted."

My heart sank when the two of them settled down at their desks in the dorm to work on their laptops, and I wondered whether to risk going up into the loft anyway. If I was totally quiet surely they wouldn't hear me below. But how could I be quieter than a cat? We'd heard Silver easily enough. Anyway there were loads of other girls still around in the boarding house, so I knew I'd have to be patient for a bit longer. It was tempting just to tell Nicole and Antonia about Silver, but something was stopping me. I was so worried that Mrs. Pridham would get to hear about him and shoo him away for ever. No, it seemed better to keep him a secret for now. And then... And then *what*?

I couldn't keep him a secret for ever. I'd *have* to tell Mrs. Pridham sometime. But not yet. For now, I just wanted to see Silver again.

In the end I went swimming. As it was still quite early for a Sunday there was hardly anyone in the pool and I did twenty lengths without stopping, then got out. The lifeguard grinned at me as I headed for the changing room. "That was quick!"

I turned and smiled back but didn't say anything. Then I dried myself and got dressed quickly, getting more and more excited that I'd soon be seeing Silver. It didn't take me a minute to dry my hair, because it's so short. I just rubbed it hard, then walked back to Forest Ash in the sun, which was better than any hairdryer.

In the dorm, Antonia and Nicole were shutting down their laptops and packing up, so my twenty lengths had filled the time perfectly.

"Oh, you've been swimming!" said Nicole. "Are there many in the pool?"

I shook my head. "Only one Year Eight when I got out."

"Shall we?" said Antonia, turning to Nicole.

Nicole broke into a grin. "Good idea of yours, Bry. See you then!"

They both grabbed their swimming things and a few seconds later they were out of the dorm. I didn't know whether the Year Nines were in their room and neither did I know whether Matron or Miss Stevenson, our assistant housemistress, or worse, Mrs. Pridham were around, but I couldn't wait any longer to see Silver.

I took the tissue with the piece of chicken out of the back of my bottom drawer and eyed it sadly. It was dry and starting to go hard and curl at the edges. As I stuffed it in my pocket and grabbed the plastic tub, I told myself that a stray cat wouldn't be fussy about what it ate. It'd be grateful for anything. I'd got my plastic water bottle so I'd be able to fill the tub once I was up there. But the most important thing was to move really carefully. If Silver was there, I didn't want him to fly off the moment I appeared.

I must have been walking much faster than usual along the landing, because I almost bumped into Matron, who was coming out of her room, her mobile to her ear.

"All right, Bryony?" She flashed her usual bright smile, and I gulped and nodded. "Stupid thing!" she said under her breath as she hurried past me. "Never any signal here!"

I held my breath and rushed round the corner, then ducked into the cleaning room, closing the door behind me and feeling like a criminal. Inside it was even too dark to see where the light switch was, so I groped my way towards the staircase that led up to the loft, and once I was on the bottom stair I felt a lovely excitement come rushing in.

Please let Silver be here, I repeated over and over in my mind as I started making those kissy sounds that people do to encourage cats to come to them. Then when I came to the top stair I changed it. "Silver," I called in the quietest sing-song voice. I wasn't going to risk frightening him away by walking across the loft, so I stayed close to the top of the stairs, and began to pour water into the plastic tub from my bottle.

I felt as though I was walking a tightrope that had worn down to a single thread; I mustn't let myself break it and neither must I fall off. And yet as I tore the chicken into little pieces and put it beside the tub, I somehow sensed that Silver was there, around the corner, listening and maybe wondering.

My voice was as thin and lilting as I could make it. "Silver! Come on!" Then I sat down cross-legged and waited in patient silence, my eyes fixed on the far wall. *Please let him be here.*

After a couple of minutes my patience was rewarded, because a thin silver-grey face appeared. Anna told me that cats don't like to see wide eyes because in the cat world it's narrowing the eyes that's a sign of friendship, and I could definitely remember Lana doing that. So I blinked a few times in slow motion while I kept murmuring Silver's name. Then, very gently, I picked up a piece of the chicken and did the kissy noises again. It was tempting to throw the chicken towards him, but I thought even that might scare him away. Instead, I played my waiting game again, and, after at least a minute (which is a long time when you're just waiting), I had an even bigger reward, because Silver began to pad over to me.

"Good, Silver. Good boy," I whispered over and over. And I tried to stay completely still. "Good boy... There you are..." I was holding my breath now, because he was so close to me I could have reached out and touched him, but I knew I mustn't, however tempting it was. He was staring at the water in the little tub. And then he dipped his head and seemed to smell it. A moment later his tongue came out and he lapped away at it until there was not a drop left. His big eyes gazed back at me and it felt as though he was asking for more. I thought I might scare him away if I unscrewed the water bottle, though, so I made some more kissy noises instead, and still he kept his eyes fixed on me. I know cats have no expressions on their faces, but it truly felt as though he was imploring me.

"Good boy," I murmured again, then slowly, slowly, I stretched out my hand towards his face and felt his breath on my fingers as he sniffed.

It was such a lovely surprise when he pushed his cheek against my hand and began to purr. It made me bolder and I stroked him properly, which he seemed to love, because he twisted and turned his head like mad, as though he couldn't get enough.

"Silver, look, chicken!" I gently picked up a piece and he sniffed it, then drew back, so I put it on the floor and in an instant he'd grabbed it and begun to gnaw at it. He didn't want to take it from my hand, of course. I should have realized that. He's not a dog, after all. As he tucked into the other little pieces of chicken, I poured more water into the tub, and in no time at all he'd lapped up the entire contents of my water bottle. It was true it was only a small one, but all the same he must have been really thirsty.

"Sorry, I don't have any more, Silver. But I'll bring you some next time I come. And more chicken too. Or whatever I can manage to steal from supper."

And as I talked and rubbed his head, he came closer, and then surprised me by stepping cautiously onto my lap. So I bent my head and he rubbed his face into my neck, which felt lovely and made me wish that he really could be my pet. My own special, *secret* pet.

Chapter Five

We were hanging around outside waiting for the bell for the start of afternoon school. It was French first.

"Did any of you manage to do the French prep?" Sasha asked.

"No," said Emily flatly. "But then…what's new?" She turned her palms up and tipped her head to one side with an innocent look on her face that was so funny we all burst out laughing.

Personally I couldn't raise any enthusiasm for French or ICT that followed. All I could think about was seeing Silver after school. I still hadn't told the others about him – I hadn't even told Emily I'd been back – because I knew they'd all want to see him and it would frighten him off if loads of people suddenly appeared. No, it was best he got used to me first.

"I've only just understood the thing about making adjectives agree with nouns," Emily went on, "but now I've got to make verbs agree as well! *Passé, composé*? What's that about?"

Antonia was still laughing as she tried to explain. "Well it's only certain verbs that have to agree."

Emily made herself go cross-eyed and we all laughed again.

"Right, listen," said Antonia, determined to get Emily to understand. "Suppose you want to say… er…'Nadia went to see Mrs. Pridham'…"

"Which she *did*, by the way," added Nicole, "but that's got nothing to do with it."

"Ssh! I'm confused!" said Emily.

"Sorry," said Nicole.

"Okay, 'Nadia went…' is *Nadia est allée* and you have to put the extra *e* on *allée* because Nadia is a girl."

Half of me was listening to what Antonia was saying, but the other half of my mind couldn't stop thinking about what Nicole had just said. Nadia was one of the Year Nines from the other room with the attic directly above them. I was probably being stupid. There were loads of reasons why Nadia might have gone to see Mrs. Pridham, but I just had to be sure.

"So Nadia...went to see Mrs. Pridham, did she?" I asked, doing my best to grin at Nicole as though I was joking about the number of times Antonia and Emily were repeating that sentence.

"Yes, the Year Nines heard that...noise again yesterday morning and it freaked them out a bit, but Mr. Monk's going to investigate and if it's a mouse or a rat he'll probably put poison down or something. That's what Nadia said anyway."

"What!" I couldn't help the massive exclamation that came out of me. It made everyone turn to me with shock in their eyes – everyone except Emily, that is, who was looking at me in horror.

My throat felt tight. Silver was starving. I'd only just got him to trust a human being and to take food from one. He'd think Mr. Monk was offering more and he wouldn't be able to resist eating it. And then he'd die. And it would be my fault for encouraging him to trust humans in the first place. If only I could rush back to Forest Ash, race up to the loft and get rid of the poison right now. Except it might be too late already.

The bell went as I was having that terrible thought, but it didn't make me abandon the idea. So what if I was late for French? Madame Poulain was the least strict teacher at Silver Spires. I could make some excuse.

"We'd better go," said Sasha, setting off in the direction of the language labs with Izzy. Nicole and Antonia followed behind, but I hung back with Emily, and began whispering to her urgently as soon as the others were out of earshot.

"I've got to try and save Silver," I said.

She looked at me sharply, then her face softened. "Ah, you've named the cat. Bry, you mustn't get attached. There's no way he's going to be able to stay in the boarding house."

I ignored that. "It might not be too late. Mr. Monk might not have got round to going up to the loft yet. Or Silver might not have gone in there."

"But what will you do?"

"I just want to check he's okay. I'm going to go right now. Can you tell the others I left my ICT stuff behind by mistake."

"You can't just—"

"Hello, girls!" came a voice from just behind us. "Aren't we lucky with this beautiful English sunshine!"

69

Emily and I turned to see Madame Poulain and Mrs. Lawson, the ICT teacher walking along together.

I thought I ought to speak straight away. "I've just realized I've left my ICT answer sheet behind, Mrs. Lawson. Is it okay if I rush back and get it, Madame Poulain? We've got ICT after French, you see."

"No, don't worry," said Mrs. Lawson. "It's not vital. We'll work together on the answers in the lesson."

I could have kicked myself. I shouldn't have said anything. Now I'd lost my chance to go back to Forest Ash before the end of school. Emily bit her lip and gave me a fleeting, pitying glance. And we walked on in silence.

All afternoon I felt terrible. Like a murderer. What would I do if I found Silver lying dead up in the attic? I knew I'd cry and cry, because he felt like my very own secret treasure, and I'd blame myself entirely for his death.

The moment the end-of-school bell went I flew back to Forest Ash, wondering whether the time had come to tell Mrs. Pridham about Silver. She was just coming out of her flat with Matron as I rushed in through the front door.

"My goodness, someone's in a hurry!" she said.

And in the two seconds it took me to cross the hall I imagined her reaction if I *did* tell her. First she'd be worried about the rat poison, and would probably get Mr. Monk to go up there and take it away immediately, because she wouldn't want to harm a cat. But then she'd probably ask him to shoo Silver off, muttering about cheeky stray cats. No, there was no way I could risk telling her the truth.

"Just think, Mrs. Pridham," Matron was saying, a smile playing about her eyes, "if I rushed around like Bryony I wouldn't have to bother with my diet!"

Mrs. Pridham laughed as Matron hurried over to me. "Let's see if I can keep up with you on the stairs, Bryony!"

My heart sank. How could I go up to the attic with Matron on my heels? But I couldn't be so rude as to race off without her so we walked upstairs together and I went into the dorm and flopped on my bed. I'd leave it a few minutes before I risked sneaking along to the cleaning room. While I was waiting I concentrated on straining my ears for any sounds at all, but it was completely silent. And it stayed that way, until Emily suddenly came crashing into the dorm followed by the others.

"Oh, Bry! Are you okay?" asked Sasha, the concern back on her face at the sight of me flat out on my bed.

Emily and I exchanged a look and I decided in that second that I must tell the others about Silver. They were standing very still, watching me carefully, not used to me looking sad, or acting dramatically. It was no wonder I'd shocked them all so much.

I sat up and sighed. "Truth talk, guys," was all I said.

"Yes, of course," said Antonia, who had invented the expression and actually the whole idea of truth talks, way back in the first term when her English hadn't been so good. We'd kept the name *Truth talk* because it said exactly what it was. Basically, if anyone in the group felt the need to share something important with the others, we all piled onto their bed and listened while they talked, then tried to make them feel better.

It felt funny watching the others climb my ladder and squash themselves on the bed, because this was the first time I'd ever been the one to call a truth talk. Once they were all sitting silently, watching me with big eyes, I began in my usual straightforward way.

"That noise you heard in the night, Izzy, is a cat."

"A cat!" said Izzy in a faint squeak, as though she didn't want to interrupt me but couldn't help her surprise slipping out.

"I went up to the loft to investigate and thought I'd seen a squirrel," I carried on. "But Ems came with me the second time and that's when we saw it was definitely a cat. The third time I took him some chicken and water, because he looks thin and hungry. He gets in and out through the window. I decided to keep him a secret in case you all wanted to see him, because I was worried that would frighten him away for ever. And..."

I stopped abruptly. What I was about to say was too private. How could I explain why Silver was so precious to me?

"She's got attached to the cat," Emily helped me out.

"I've...called it Silver," I managed to say. "Only now I'm scared that..."

"Oh no! The poison!" said Nicole, clapping both hands to her mouth and looking horrified.

"What are you going to do?" asked Antonia quietly.

I shrugged. "I'm going to the attic. I just want to see Silver alive. I was waiting until Matron was out of the way."

Nicole covered her eyes with her hands as though she couldn't bear the thought of what I might find. Then she quickly took them away and asked if I wanted anyone with me for moral support.

I shook my head. "It's okay." My mouth was dry as I left the dorm. "Tell me afterwards if you could hear me moving about up there."

I didn't pass a soul on the landing. I shut the cleaning room door behind me without a sound and crept towards the stairs in the darkness. At the top, I hardly dared look around me. My heart pounded horribly as I stood completely still for a few seconds, wondering what to do.

"Silver," I whispered in a breathy voice as I began to tiptoe across the floor.

So far he hadn't been the kind of cat that miaowed, but still the answering silence made me tense up. And then suddenly I spotted something on the floor beside the water tank that hadn't been there the day before. It was a plastic container about twenty centimetres long and maybe ten wide, with tiny holes in the side of it and something sticking up out of it, like a little ledge with some... chocolate on it. I peered at the container, and when it dawned on me what it was, I felt a bubble of laughter rising up inside me. This was a humane rat trap. There wasn't any poison. Good old Mr. Monk. The very worst that could happen to Silver would be that he might get his paw stuck in it, and I somehow thought he was too clever for that.

Even though the loft felt totally deserted and Silver probably wasn't there, I just had to make sure because I really wanted to see for myself that he was all right, so I tiptoed on towards the corner. As I'd thought, there was no sign of my precious cat. He was probably out hunting or trying to find water from somewhere, which wouldn't be easy on such a hot day. What a shame I hadn't brought any more water for him. *I'll come back after supper*, I thought to myself, *and bring plenty of titbits too*. I couldn't wait to tell the others about the trap, so they could stop worrying. Especially poor Nicole.

I was on the point of leaving the loft, though, when I got the shock of my life, because two things happened at the same time. Silver crept in through the window. And footsteps sounded on the stairs. Heavy footsteps.

I was frozen to the spot for a second, my brain working in a frenzy to make a decision. I was certain that this wasn't one of my friends, because they would have called up to tell me not to panic. No, it had to be an adult. But the footsteps sounded too heavy even for Matron or Mrs. Pridham. So it had to be Mr. Monk.

Mr. Monk! There was no way I could let him catch me up here. I went right round the corner and pressed myself against the wall, praying that Silver would go quickly before he was seen. It was obvious from the way his wiry body had stiffened that the noise on the stairs had frightened him, and after only a second of seeming frozen like a cat statue, he leaped back up onto the window ledge and disappeared.

From my hiding place I could hear Mr. Monk take a few steps into the attic, then stop. I guessed he was checking the trap. A moment later he took a few more steps in my direction. I could hear him muttering to himself, but the only two words I could make out were "...fix that". Then there was the sound of the window shutting and opening again, more muttering, and finally Mr. Monk's footsteps heading back towards the stairs, followed by the shuffly thuds that his feet made on each step.

I realized I'd been holding my breath for ages, and let it out in a long slow sigh of relief as I crept out of my hiding place. And that's when I noticed for the first time that the catch on the window was broken.

Chapter Six

Emily grabbed my wrist and practically yanked me into the dorm the moment I'd opened the door. "We only really heard you at the end, Bry. It was like you'd forgotten to creep or something. We hardly heard a thing before that."

Then Nicole started to gabble. "But what happened? Was Silver there? *Please* tell me Silver was there."

"It wasn't me you heard. It was Mr. Monk..."

They all gasped. "Mr. Monk! Did you manage to avoid him?" asked Izzy.

Emily jumped in with another question before

I could answer. "Did he see Silver?"

"I don't think so. Silver came in through the window just as Mr. Monk was coming up the stairs, but the poor thing turned and bolted at the sound of his footsteps. And Mr. Monk didn't notice me because I was round the corner out of sight. He didn't come in as far as that, thank goodness. But the good news is that there wasn't any poison. He's put one of those humane traps down with a bit of chocolate as bait."

"So that's what he was doing then," said Emily. "Checking the trap. You're supposed to check those humane ones every day."

"But the bad thing," I went on, "is that the catch on the window is broken. That's how Silver's been able to come and go. Up the trellis to the roof, then through the window. Only now Mr. Monk's spotted it, because I heard him muttering about getting it fixed." I sighed heavily. "And then what'll happen to poor Silver?"

"Maybe you've just got to risk telling Mrs. P, Bry." Sasha's face looked so sympathetic. "She'll find Silver a good home, I'm sure."

I knew Sasha was right, but even though it was selfish of me, I was starting to dread the thought of Silver leaving Forest Ash.

"I want to see him!" said Antonia, suddenly hunching her shoulders excitedly like a little girl.

"Me too," said Izzy.

"We'll frighten him away for good if we all go trooping up there," said Emily firmly. "Let Bry go on her own a couple more times until Silver's used to her."

"And what about when Mr. Monk's fixed the window?" asked Nicole, her face in a heavy frown.

"Maybe we can find a secret, sheltered place somewhere outside, and keep him there," said Izzy.

There was a dull silence and I guessed the others were trying to think, like I was, of where on earth we could possibly keep a cat in secret. And anyway, we'd all be going home for the summer holidays soon. What then?

After supper it's prep and I thought this would be the perfect time to go up to the loft. Everyone would be occupied, and even if the Year Nines were working in their room, I knew now that they weren't likely to hear me. It must have been when Silver jumped from the window ledge or ran across the loft that the sound could be heard from below. Also, at night-time it's as though the silence grows a deeper layer.

During the day there's hardly ever any time when you're completely silent in your dorm. There's movement and chatter and music.

Prep is just like homework. The Year Sevens and Eights have to work for an hour in silence, supervised by Mrs. Pridham, Miss Stevenson or Matron, and it's all very serious. We're definitely not supposed to be late, especially when Miss Stevenson's on duty, because, although she's the youngest member of Forest Ash boarding staff, she's also probably the strictest.

Emily and I rushed through supper and raced back to Forest Ash, each carrying bits of battered fish in our pockets, wrapped up in tissue. In the dorm we carefully peeled off the batter and left it in my drawer, because we didn't dare chuck it in the bin. We're not allowed any food in the dorms so I'd have to get rid of it the next day. I got my plastic tub and my water bottle, and sneaked along the corridor, round the corner and into the cleaning room as quickly as I could.

I tiptoed up the stairs and across the floor towards Silver's corner, only giving the mousetrap the smallest of glances just to check it was empty. I was desperately hoping that Silver would be there, but in my heart I must have thought he wouldn't be, because it gave me a shock when I found him sitting snugly on a pile of dust sheets, looking perfectly serene. I felt so happy that he trusted me and didn't immediately bolt out of the window. I bent down and stroked him, scratching between his ears and talking in whispers as he pushed his head against my fingers and closed his eyes. I could tell he loved his little massage.

Somewhere in the back of my mind a memory was stirring. I'd stroked another cat like this, and the cat had purred and snuggled closer to me just like Silver was doing now. Fellini? No, I'd never scratched Fellini's head. In fact I'd never even stroked Fellini. He wasn't the kind of cat that looked as though he wanted to be stroked, the way he turned his back on people and plonked himself in the middle of a cushion, then stared around as if to say, *Look at me! I'm the king!*

So if it wasn't Fellini, it must have been Lana. I hadn't had any memory of stroking Lana until now and it filled me with a mixture of sadness and confusion. I looked at Silver's soft head and for a moment it was just as though the years had gone rolling away and I was a little girl again stroking Lana. I swallowed, feeling my throat hurting at the memory. But then, as quickly as the memory had come, it dissolved and I was back in the present with Silver.

When I put the fish in front of him he attacked it straight away, only breaking off to lap the water that I poured into the tub.

"Good boy," I kept murmuring, sitting down beside him and hugging my knees. I couldn't wait for the others to see him now he was so much calmer and more trusting.

Then I looked at my watch and realized I had to go or I'd be late for prep, so I got up and said goodbye to my lovely new pet as I walked away from him. It was an awful wrench, almost like I was saying goodbye to Lana all over again, especially when he narrowed his eyes at me and purred.

"Sorry, Silver. I'll be back as soon as poss. Promise."

It was as I was munching my last bit of toast at breakfast the next day that I suddenly remembered I'd left Silver's water tub up in the loft.

"But if you left it round the corner, there's no chance of Mr. Monk seeing it," Emily said, with a wave of her hand. "He probably only pops his head up at the top of the stairs, just enough to check whether a mouse has been caught in the trap, and that's it."

"And he might not even bother to do that," said Nicole, "because Mrs. Pridham asked me this morning whether any of us had heard anything from the loft recently, and I said we hadn't heard a single thing for ages."

Those words really cheered me up. "Oh, well done, Nicole!" Except that straight afterwards I remembered that Mr. Monk had another reason to go up into the loft. He was going to fix the window, wasn't he.

"I can't wait to see Silver," said Sasha, her eyes brightening. "When shall we go?"

"After school?" suggested Izzy.

I thought that was probably the best plan, but fear was gathering inside me again. When Mr. Monk had fixed the catch, he'd leave the window closed. I hated to think about poor little Silver not being able to get in. He'd wonder what had happened.

As the day went on I grew more and more anxious and finally, at the end of lessons, I rushed back to Forest Ash and practically bashed into Mr. Monk as I ran across the hall.

"Oh...sorry," I stumbled, feeling embarrassed about seeing Mr. Monk now.

"Someone's in a bit of a rush!" he laughed.

I just smiled and hurried on, but he called out to me as I leaped up the stairs two at a time. "You're one of the girls in Emerald, aren't you?"

I stopped.

"One of the ones who got disturbed by mysterious noises in the night?"

"I...yes...we heard a mouse or something..." I said, turning to face him.

He chuckled as though it was a great joke. "Well, let me tell you, that was no mouse. I went up there to check the trap I set, and there was this cat! Sniffing the chocolate I'd put out for bait. I couldn't believe my eyes!"

I felt as though I should be saying something but I had to force the words out, I was so filled with alarm. "A cat?" was all I managed.

"Don't look so worried. It won't be coming back. I've shooed it away good and proper."

"Oh...right..."

"Catch is broken on the window. That's how it got in, cheeky thing. I'll get round to mending it one of these days, but you don't need to worry about that cat coming back. Oh no!"

"How do you know it won't come back?" I asked carefully.

Mr. Monk shook his head. "I reckon I scared it enough not to come back when I clapped my hands and chased it off."

"I'd better go," I muttered, as I carried on walking up the stairs, feeling my spirits sinking with every step I took.

The next four days were awful. Emily said I was torturing myself by wandering round the grounds in search of Silver and sneaking up to the loft so often. But I couldn't help just checking that a miracle hadn't happened and Silver had returned. I remember the first time I went up, just after Mr. Monk had told me about shooing him away, I'd stared at the pile of dust sheets and felt such pity rising up inside me I'd honestly thought it might choke me. I'd told myself it was stupid. It was only a cat. I never could have kept him. But the past wouldn't stop creeping into the present and all the sadness I'd felt when Lana had died kept on welling up inside me.

The feeling still hadn't left me four days later.

I suppose I should have counted myself lucky that Mr. Monk obviously didn't spot the tub, and it looked like he'd forgotten about the catch too, because it still wasn't fixed. Every time I went up

I took a little plastic bag with some fresh food and left it tucked right round the corner so there was no way Mr. Monk would find it. The food was never touched, though. The first time I looked at the water I got excited because it definitely seemed as if some had gone. But Nicole said it would have evaporated because of the heat in the loft. I could tell she and the others were a bit sad not to have ever met Silver, but no one actually said anything directly about it. They probably didn't want to add to my depression.

On Sunday we woke up to a very grey and overcast day. By lunchtime it was pouring down. We all felt good though, because we spent the morning catching up on the work we'd missed through lazing about in the sun so often over the last couple of weeks. Mrs. Pridham asked me whether we'd heard any more noises from above and I said no, nothing at all, but she frowned and said "Hmm, that's a bit of a puzzle because the Year Nines say they've definitely heard something – not at night-time, but during the day."

I felt guilty then, because although I wasn't exactly lying to Mrs. Pridham, it still felt like a lie. And I was sorry for scaring the Year Nines too.

I made a decision at that moment. I would just go up to the loft one more time to see if Silver was there and if he wasn't, I would try and forget about him. When I told Emily she seemed relieved.

"Bryony's only going to check the loft one last time," she told the others at lunchtime.

Everyone nodded and started telling me how sensible that was, and how I'd soon forget about Silver, and I realized they'd all been getting anxious about the number of times I'd risked going up there.

As it happened there was no opportunity to go up for the rest of that day, because there were so many people in Forest Ash on our floor. One of the Year Nines was ill and had a constant stream of visitors all afternoon and evening.

So it wasn't till morning break on Monday that I finally managed to sneak along to the cleaning room and whizz upstairs. I couldn't even wait till lunchtime, because this turned out to be the day that Sasha's old school friend, Hannah, was coming for her introductory day. Mrs. Pridham knew about the connection between Hannah and Sasha and thought it would be nice for Hannah if we six showed her our dorm after lunch.

"I think she's going to feel rather lost being the

only one having her introductory day today," she said, "and I'm sure she'd love to see a dorm and spend some time with you girls."

Emily and I had exchanged a look when Mrs. P said that, because we were thinking that, if Hannah was with us, I wouldn't be able to go and see if Silver was there, which was why I'd finished up rushing over to Forest Ash during morning break.

The first thing I noticed was that the mousetrap had gone. And after that I realized that the window had been fixed and was closed tight, which explained why it was hotter than usual.

So that was definitely it then. Silver couldn't come back now and I may as well get used to the idea. I'd got into the habit of taking off my shoes and creeping as soundlessly as possible, but this time, although I took my shoes off, I didn't make any real effort to tread carefully. I just walked across the loft, waiting for the disappointment to hit me.

"Silver..." It came out in a half-hearted voice. I didn't even know why I was bothering.

But then my heart skipped a beat, because there he was, lying on his side on the pile of dust sheets, and I so wanted to bend down and pick him up and cuddle him and stroke him, but I knew I mustn't do anything to scare him.

"Oh Silver! You're here!" I said in a cracked voice, feeling my throat hurt because I was so happy.

He blinked at me slowly and didn't move at all. I did, though. I went straight to the window and opened it. I didn't want Silver to be trapped in the loft, and in this boiling hot atmosphere he might suffocate or something if he didn't have a bit of air.

"There!" I said quietly. "That's better, isn't it!"

Still he didn't move a muscle. And neither did I, because I was confused. There was something different about him. What was it? It wasn't his face. Was it his body? Maybe he'd finally started to put some weight on with all the food I'd been giving him. I bent down and stroked him gently and he started purring straight away. I noticed he'd eaten the food from yesterday and drunk all the water too, so I quickly poured more into the tub and unwrapped today's food package, then went back to stroking him. He slowly stretched and rolled onto his back. And that's when I noticed definite teats on his chest, and gasped. Silver wasn't a *he* at all, but a *she*!

Chapter Seven

"Ems, I think I've discovered something. Only I need you to check."

My friends were waiting for me at the top of the little side lane that leads down to the humanities block where we were about to have history.

"What?" they all wanted to know.

"Was he there?" asked Nicole, looking excited.

I nodded. "Only I think...*think*...that *he* is a *she*!"

It took a moment for my words to sink in, then Sasha asked how I could tell. "I don't know much about cats," she said, blushing a bit, "but is it kind of...obvious?"

"The thing is," I said, in my usual straightforward way, because I never feel embarrassed about things like this, "I think she's got teats."

Emily had set off towards the humanities block, following Nicole and Antonia, but she stopped suddenly and turned to face me when I said that. "Teats aren't usually that obvious on cats actually, Bryony, unless…"

"Unless what?"

"Nothing."

"Oh come on, Ems! What?" I was getting exasperated.

"I'll come and look at her after school," she promised.

I nodded. "Thanks, Ems. And…there's something else…"

"What?"

"Mr. Monk's fixed the catch so I opened the window, because I didn't want Silver to be trapped. Also it's boiling hot in there. She'd roast with the window shut."

"What if Mr. Monk notices the window is open?" asked Izzy as we went into the humanities block.

"I don't think he'll go up there now he's fixed the catch and taken the mousetrap away," I replied.

"No, I mean, what if he sees it from outside?"

A little alarm bell rang somewhere deep inside me, but I ignored it as soon as I realized Mr. Monk would have to be round the side of the building looking right up to the roof to even notice the window.

We were about to troop into our history class when Mrs. Pridham came into the block with Hannah and smiled round at us.

"Oh good, I've caught you just in time. This is Hannah, girls, and she'll be joining us at Silver Spires next year."

"Hi!" said Sasha warmly. "I really like your hair! You look so different with it short!"

Hannah thanked her and gave us all a nervous half-smile. I didn't think I'd ever seen anyone look so anxious.

"We're on a bit of a Silver Spires tour at the moment," went on Mrs. Pridham in an over-the-top cheerful voice that she didn't often use. I thought she was probably trying to make up for Hannah's quietness. "But there's a lot to take in, isn't there?"

Hannah nodded, but didn't say anything. She must have been really shy. She was wearing light-coloured cut-off trousers, a very plain brown and white top and soft brown shoes that were the nearest thing you can get to trainers without actually being trainers. I don't usually notice what people are wearing but I did this time, because I was remembering how I'd struggled to decide what to wear this time last year for my own introductory day. Anna had thought I should wear a skirt but, as I never ever wear skirts normally, and the only one I'd got in my wardrobe made me look about seven and a half, I'd been dead against that. I'd wanted to wear jeans and trainers, and in the end we'd compromised on cut-offs and some shoes that were almost trainers.

The main thing you noticed about Hannah, though, was definitely her hair. It was even shorter than mine, and a lovely dark coppery colour, whereas mine's almost black. I wondered whether she was a tomboy, like me, and was feeling out of her depth, because there were so many girls with long hair around the place, and everyone seemed so loud and confident. I knew that feeling and I couldn't help feeling sorry for her.

"Okay, girls," Mrs. Pridham was saying, still in her over-the-top bright voice, "I know you have to go into your next lesson now, but I'll bring Hannah along to the dining hall at about ten to one, and then she can sit at your table, okay?"

"Yes, fine!" said Sasha straight away. She smiled

at Hannah. "We'll look after you, don't worry."

Mrs. Pridham beamed. "Great! And you'll bring her over to Forest Ash after lunch and show her round?"

"Yes, of course!" said Sasha.

"Do you want some water, Hannah?" asked Izzy, grabbing a tumbler.

"Yes please," said Hannah. She was so polite, even with Sasha.

Mrs. Pridham had brought her along to the dining hall, as she'd said she would, at ten to one on the dot. My friends and I were all in the lunch queue, and we'd asked Hannah what she wanted, because there was a choice of chicken or sausage salad, or you could have pizza and chips, or pizza and salad, and you could choose plain sliced bread or you could have a roll.

"I'll just have what you're having," said Hannah in her quiet voice.

"We're all having different things," said Emily.

"Have the chicken salad!" said Sasha. "It's delicious."

So that's what Hannah did but I noticed she didn't eat very much. I guessed she was too nervous.

Between the six of us we asked her lots of questions and learned that she lived in a village called Rivers Mead that was about fifteen miles from where Sasha lives. She had two much older brothers, one at uni and one who was going to uni next year. She liked reading, writing poetry and stories and listening to music, and she'd never been to a boarding school before. By the time we got on to pudding she was definitely more relaxed, because she and Sasha had been discussing their old teachers at primary school, and she'd actually laughed when Sasha told us all that for the whole of Year One she'd thought her teacher, Miss Isworth, was called Mrs. Worth.

"Are you nervous about coming here?" Emily asked when she'd just helped herself to seconds of the pudding.

Hannah just nodded.

"You do get used to it quite quickly," I told her. "I missed my family like mad at first, but then I met all my lovely friends, and just kind of got into a routine."

"And the food's really good here," Emily changed the conversation dramatically. "Like this yummy rhubarb and honey tart! Made with home-grown rhubarb!" she added proudly.

Hannah smiled at that and we talked about the garden a bit until we'd all finished eating.

Back at Forest Ash, Mrs. Pridham asked Hannah if she'd enjoyed her lunch, then told her she was looking forward to having a nice cup of tea and a chat with her after she'd visited Emerald, so upstairs we all trooped.

Hannah seemed to love looking round our dorm. Sasha and Antonia were talking through every single little detail about where we kept things and what happened at night-time. But my mind was wandering back to Silver, and my ears were pricked up for any sounds that might be coming from above.

It was when Sasha was looking out of the window and talking about the ash trees in the distance that Hannah suddenly said, "What was that?"

Her face was very still and I could tell she was listening.

My heart raced as Emily glanced at me, and Sasha said, "I didn't hear anything."

"There it is again!" Hannah was looking up at the ceiling. She must have had amazing hearing because, like Sasha, I hadn't heard a sound. Then suddenly she tensed up, crossing her arms in front of her and making them white where her fingers were digging in. "Forest Ash doesn't have a ghost, does it?"

"No, of course not," I said quickly.

"You're not keeping it from me to stop me worrying, are you?"

"No, there's definitely no ghost, Hannah, honestly," Sasha assured her.

"But I'm sure I heard something." She suddenly stopped and looked up to the ceiling again. "Wh-what is it if it's not a ghost?"

Her eyes were glistening by then and Sasha gave her a hug. "It's all right, Hannah."

"I know I'm being stupid," she gulped. "I've got myself in a state. I just don't think I'll be very good at living away from home. I must be the only girl in the world who's so pathetic."

"You're not pathetic!" said Nicole.

"And you're definitely not the only person to worry about boarding. Everyone feels homesick at first," added Antonia.

"My mum always says it's only fear of the unknown that makes us scared," added Nicole.

A memory of what Katy had said at Pets' Place suddenly flashed through my mind. She'd been talking about having her rabbit, Buddy, at school.

It stopped me panicking at the thought of what lay ahead in this big unknown place.

"Do you have a pet you could bring to school, like a guinea pig or a rabbit?" I asked her.

She shook her head, but I wasn't certain she'd even taken in what I'd asked her, because of what she said next. "There could be a ghost up there that you haven't come across yet."

I glanced at Emily and she nodded, knowing instantly how my mind was working.

"Hannah," I said, "I'll prove to you that it's not a ghost. Come with me. There's nothing to worry about."

Sasha smiled and Izzy said, "You're going to love this, Hannah!"

And I thought how lovely and understanding my friends were, not to mind that Hannah would be seeing Silver before they would.

"I'll come too, for identification purposes!" said Emily, smiling mysteriously, which made Hannah's eyes turn curious through her tears.

"Where are we going?" she asked as we walked along the landing.

"In here," I said, diving into the cleaning room. "Quick! We're not exactly supposed to be here."

"Oh...are you sure...?" But she stopped mid-sentence

and I saw a glimmer of fear come into her eyes as we started to climb the narrow staircase up to the loft.

"You have to creep really softly," Emily told her.

Hannah nodded, clinging to us like a shadow.

"I'm going to show you what was making the noise you heard," I whispered. "No one knows about it except us six. But you can share our secret."

I didn't think it was possible for anyone's eyes to open as wide as Hannah's did at that moment. We tiptoed across the loft and round the corner to where Silver lay contentedly on her dust sheets and Hannah gasped, then clapped a hand to her mouth as if even that gasp might have been too loud.

"Ah...she's so sweet!"

I saw a completely different Hannah then. The frightened Hannah was gone. In her place was a gentle girl who was suddenly taken up with my precious cat, bending down and stretching out her fingers as Silver blinked at her slowly.

"What's her name, Bryony?"

"Silver."

"That's a good name. Like Silver Spires. That means she truly belongs here."

I smiled, then felt a stab of sadness knowing that could never happen.

"How did you find her?"

"We heard noises from our dorm, just like you did, and everyone thought it might be a mouse or a bird or something. But I thought it was too soft and smooth for a mouse, and I started imagining we had a Forest Ash ghost, so I came up here to investigate one day and I couldn't believe it when I saw Silver. It's like she's chosen our loft specially. I...I haven't told Mrs. Pridham, in case she shoos her away."

"I wouldn't have told her either," said Hannah, nodding thoughtfully. "Except that Silver looks just like my cat did when she was pregnant."

So then it was my turn to gasp. I turned to Emily, who hadn't said anything so far.

She bent down and examined Silver carefully. "Yes, she is. That's what I was going to say earlier, Bry – that teats only really show on cats when they're going to have kittens."

"Kittens?" It was a stupid thing to say. Obviously she wasn't going to have puppies, but I was so surprised. "When?"

Emily shrugged. "I'm not sure. But she looks... settled. It could be soon."

None of us spoke for at least twenty seconds while two thoughts twined around and around each other in my mind.

It would be so wonderful to have Silver and her kittens at Forest Ash.

Mrs. Pridham would go absolutely mad if she knew that a wild cat was living here in the attic; never in a million years would she allow Silver to stay.

Three loud taps that seemed to come from somewhere below nearly made me jump out of my skin. Hannah tensed up and her hand shot to her mouth. "What was that?"

Then it came again, exactly the same. And I suddenly realized it must be one of the others tapping something against the ceiling in our dorm as a warning.

"There might be someone coming," I told Hannah. "Keep out of sight. If it's Mr. Monk he won't look round here."

Hannah looked at her watch. "You don't think the others are just warning you about the time?"

So then I looked at my own watch. "Yes, you're right. I'd forgotten all about afternoon school!"

Back in the dorm, Emily told the others straight away about Silver being pregnant. They all seemed really excited about it to begin with.

Nicole was the first to lose her smile and turn

serious. "What...will you do when the kittens are born, Bry?"

"I'm not sure," I said, sighing inside. "Mrs. Pridham would never let us keep Silver or the kittens. That's all I know."

"Doesn't she like cats?" asked Hannah quietly.

No one answered that question, because the truth was we didn't actually know whether Mrs. Pridham liked cats or not, and an idea started to form in my mind.

"Hannah," I began slowly, "Mrs. P said something about a cup of tea and a chat with you, didn't she?"

"Yes, before I go home."

"Well, I don't suppose you could somehow get the conversation round to pets. I mean, especially if you have your own cat. Maybe you can discover what Mrs. P thinks about cats in general?"

"You're a genius, Bry!" said Emily, slapping me on the back.

"Yes, she might turn out to be completely cat mad!" said Izzy, smiling.

But now I was picturing Mrs. Pridham's flat with not a cat in sight. "At least you can suss whether or not she's likely to blow a fuse when she finds out about Silver," I said, sighing on the outside this time.

Hannah laughed lightly. "I'll check out how she feels about kittens as well, shall I?"

Looking at her bright confident smile, I couldn't believe the transformation from the girl we'd met earlier in the day who'd been so fragile with worry that it looked like the tiniest thing would make her crumple.

"We'd better get going to afternoon school!" said Izzy.

So we all piled out of the dorm and made our way downstairs.

"Before I go, I'll let you know what Mrs. Pridham says about you-know-what," Hannah whispered, when we were in the hall.

"I don't think Mrs. P will let you interrupt us in lessons," I said, thinking it through, "but let's exchange mobile numbers, then you can text me."

So that's what we did.

"Thank you for…looking after me," said Hannah, looking round us all, when we'd knocked on Mrs. Pridham's door.

"That's okay. Sorry we have to fly. See you next term!" said Sasha, giving her a quick hug, before rushing off to the library for English with Izzy and Nicole. Emily, Antonia and I aren't in the top set, like the other three, and our lessons are in the

English block, which isn't quite such a trek from Forest Ash.

"Bye, Hannah!" said Antonia.

"Hurry along, girls!" interrupted Mrs. Pridham, appearing at her door. "I don't want your teachers blaming me for making you late!"

Emily and Antonia went tearing off and I was about to follow, when Hannah grabbed my hand and looked me straight in the eyes. "Thank you for sharing a little chunk of your Silver Spires life with me, Bryony," she said. "I feel so much happier now about coming here next term."

I felt quite choked up when she said that and found that I couldn't even reply, so I just nodded quickly and smiled. Mrs. Pridham was looking from one to the other of us with an expression on her face that I couldn't work out. She put her hand on Hannah's shoulder, and that seemed to prompt Hannah to let go of my hand. I turned and rushed after Emily, feeling my emotions swirling round inside me, all mixed up and heavy. I didn't look back, because I didn't want Hannah to see the tears in my eyes. She might not understand them. I didn't understand them myself. I'd have to try to work them out later when I was lying in bed. But for now I just blinked them away, because I never cry. Never.

Chapter Eight

We have to switch our phones off during lessons and if we're found with them turned on, they're automatically confiscated. That's the rule. And you don't get them back for two days, so there's no point in risking it, as the teachers do spot checks every so often. It's okay to switch them on between lessons though, and that's what I did when we were on the way to double ICT after English.

"Look, Ems, there's a message from Hannah already." I read it out to her. "*Mrs. P def not animal person but v symp so shd b ok. Tx again. Luv Han.*"

"What's 'symp'?" asked Emily.

I said the only word I could think of that started with "symp". "Sympathetic?"

"Yes, sympathetic," said Emily staring into the distance. "So Hannah's saying that Mrs. P doesn't particularly like animals but because she's a sympathetic kind of person, she should react okay to Silver. Is that it?"

I nodded slowly. We all knew that Mrs. Pridham was kind and sympathetic, but I was thinking she'd have to be the most sympathetic person under the sun to forgive us for keeping Silver a secret and for actually encouraging her to stay at Forest Ash.

As soon as school had finished, the six of us made our way back to Forest Ash, planning when would be the best time for the others to get to see Silver and trying not to think about how we should break the news to Mrs. Pridham.

"We'd better go in pairs," said Emily. "We don't want to frighten her when she's so close to giving birth. She didn't seem to mind when there was just three of us, but six might be a bit much, and if she got traumatized the kittens could be stillborn."

"Oh that's terrible!" said Nicole, and I felt my heart beating faster at the thought.

"Just think, she might have had her kittens already!" said Antonia, brightening our moods.

"How long are cats pregnant for?" asked Nicole.

Emily pursed her lips. "I think it's eight weeks. Nothing like as long as humans anyway."

"I wonder what the father looks like," said Sasha. "I hope he's completely different from Silver, then the kittens will come out all patchy and fab."

I was listening to my friends chattering away, but I couldn't join in, because I kept thinking that I needed to tell Mrs. Pridham about the pregnant cat in our attic, but I was dreading her reaction. What if she made Mr. Monk get rid of Silver *and* her kittens? I was clinging like mad to what Hannah had said, and hoping that Mrs. P would at least let us keep Silver and then advertise the kittens so they would go to good homes. But I felt heavy inside, full of worry about what might happen.

"Look, isn't that Mrs. P?" Izzy suddenly said as we neared Forest Ash. "Who's that she's with?"

"It's Mr. Pridham, isn't it?" Sasha answered. "But what are they looking at?"

We hardly ever see Mr. Pridham at Forest Ash because he works such long hours and isn't anything to do with the school at all. He's a very nice man, quite quiet and gentle. If he comes across any of us he always says, "Hello there!" and breaks into a big smile, as though he knows exactly who we are, but actually we've realized he hasn't got a clue, he's just being friendly.

"And look, there's Mr. Monk walking round to join them," said Nicole.

He was. And his head was tilted back, his hand shielding his eyes from the bright sun just like Mr. and Mrs. Pridham. My heart started pounding as I realized exactly what had grabbed their attention. "Oh no! It's the attic window!"

"What about it?" asked Sasha.

"I opened it, remember. And they've noticed."

We all stopped in our tracks about twenty-five metres away from where the three adults were standing, still staring up at the window.

"Just walk straight in to Forest Ash as though it's nothing to do with us," said Emily. "They probably won't even notice us from round the side there."

So that's what we did, a stiff, silent group, walking slowly so we could eavesdrop.

"Fancy me not spotting it!" Mr. Monk was saying in a bewildered voice. "I must be going mad! I could have sworn I left it shut."

I felt myself tensing up, and beside me Emily did an over-the-top gulping noise.

"Come on!" I hissed. "Go inside."

"Oh, girls..." called Mrs. Pridham, spotting us. "Well done for making Hannah feel at home." I noticed her eyes were on me, warm and kind. "You worked some real magic on her – she was such a frightened soul before she spent that time with you."

"That's okay," Nicole called out brightly.

Then Mr. Monk suddenly said, "You girls heard any other noises from the attic lately?"

I shook my head and we all answered him together in a rushing torrent.

"No."

"Nothing."

"No."

"Not a sound."

"No we haven't."

"There can't be anything there."

The echo of our voices seemed to hang in the air. Our answers had come far too quickly. It was no wonder Mrs. Pridham was eyeing us suspiciously.

"Emily?" she said, her eyebrows raised.

I didn't get why she'd singled out Emily, until I looked at my best friend and saw that she was bright red. Then my heart pounded even harder.

"Y-yes?" replied Emily shakily.

"You look a bit uncomfortable. Is there anything you'd like to tell me?" I know I didn't imagine it – Mrs. Pridham's tone was definitely harder.

"Well, I'll be off," said Mr. Pridham, darting round the back of Forest Ash, where there's another entrance to their flat. I could tell he didn't want to get involved with whatever was about to happen. I wished I could disappear too, because I was filled with dread. Everything depended on Emily keeping her cool.

"No," she replied, turning her palms up as though Mrs. Pridham had accused her of stealing something.

"So none of you has heard any more noises coming from the attic recently?" Mr. Monk repeated clearly and slowly.

This time there was a pause before any of us answered. "No...we haven't..." All the certainty had left our voices. And Emily hadn't said a word, as though she didn't trust herself to speak.

Mrs. Pridham walked over to us and we stood there silent and strained, waiting for the interrogation that was about to come. "Emily, do you know how this window managed to open itself?"

Suddenly I didn't think it was fair that poor Emily was being picked on, just because she's the one who goes red most easily. And I realized something else too. We were very close to being found out. So it would be better to tell the truth straight away. We'd known we'd have to tell Mrs. P in the end. And I had to be the one to do it. After all, I'm what I suppose you'd call the ringleader where Silver is concerned, so it was up to me to take responsibility and face the music.

I spoke quietly but kept my eyes on Mrs. Pridham. "*I* was the one who opened the window." I could feel five pairs of eyes boring into me and stifled gasps like mini explosions going off around me.

Mrs. Pridham's gaze left Emily and swung round to me. "You went up to the attic?"

I nodded.

"Why, might I ask?"

I didn't hesitate. And I didn't look down at all, but kept my eyes on Mrs. Pridham's, because I wasn't scared of the trouble I was in. Only scared for Silver. "To see what was making the noise."

My friends were completely silent. Waiting for the worst, I guessed.

"And what *was* making the noise, Bryony?"

"It was a cat!" chipped in Mr. Monk. "Cheeky thing. But I got rid of it, didn't I, and fixed the catch so it couldn't come back." Over his face came a slow

112

look of realization and with his next words, I saw his eyes widen even more. "I bet the pesky thing has come back!"

"And then you went up again and deliberately opened the window?" said Mrs. Pridham, entirely ignoring Mr. Monk but frowning hard at me.

Still I made myself keep my eyes on hers. "Yes, and I left food for the cat, because I felt sorry for it."

"You went and fed a mangy old stray?" Mr. Monk spluttered, as though he couldn't believe anyone would be so stupid.

I swallowed.

"You've been very deceitful," said Mrs. Pridham, lowering her voice, which sent shivers down my spine. She looked around the rest of us. "You *all* have. The Year Nines have been insisting they've heard noises and I've just shrugged off what they said as over imaginative. They've been getting themselves all wound up thinking there's a ghost up there. Do you realize how much your behaviour has upset them, Bryony?"

"Sorry."

"Is that all?"

"Bryony's not the only one. I've been up there too," said Emily in a gabble.

"And they wouldn't have gone in the first place if it hadn't been for me being so scared," added Izzy.

"Is the cat still there?" Mrs. Pridham asked, raising her voice again and fixing her sharp gaze on Emily now.

"Yes, she is," I answered quickly. "The others all wanted to tell you, but I told them not to because I thought you might...get rid of her."

"And you were right there, Bryony. I will most certainly get rid of her. We can't have stray cats living in the attic at Forest Ash. It's completely unhygienic and unacceptable."

Emily threw me the subtlest of glances, her eyebrows raised. I got her message. She was wondering whether or not we should tell Mrs. Pridham that Silver was pregnant. In a way it might explain our behaviour. But in another way, it might make us seem even more guilty in Mrs. Pridham's eyes, for not having reported something so important. I gave Emily the tiniest shake of my head when no one was looking.

Mrs. Pridham turned suddenly to Mr. Monk. "Let's deal with it, Terry. Right now."

"No, please don't..." I blurted out as the two of them strode past us.

Mrs. Pridham pushed open the Forest Ash front door and called over her shoulder, "Go to your dorm! Now!"

We all trooped upstairs, Mrs. Pridham leading the way. But Mr. Monk couldn't keep up with her. I could hear him puffing a bit, because he's quite overweight. I looked round at my friends following meekly behind and thought how they seemed to have had the fight knocked out of them. They'd given in.

But *I* hadn't. I was remembering Emily's warning about not frightening Silver and I was determined to get to her before Mrs. Pridham did, so she wouldn't be traumatized. The thought spurred me into action and I started leaping upstairs two at a time, to my friends' amazement. Mrs. Pridham was pretty surprised too, as I overtook her on the last flight.

"Bryony, go to your dorm!" she repeated in an even sterner voice, as she followed me with brisk, firm footsteps.

I ignored her, because I was on a mission now, and I rushed on, dashing along the landing and round the corner into the cleaning room.

"*Bryony!*" I didn't think I'd ever heard Mrs. Pridham use such a sharp tone of voice, but still I ignored her. All I could think about was making sure Silver was all right. I even ignored Emily's worried call. "Bry…"

Running up the steep, narrow stairs to the attic I thought I'd managed to get quite far ahead of Mrs. Pridham. I was past caring about what might happen to me after this. The only thing that mattered was Silver and her kittens. I made myself slow down to walk across the loft, my head full of thoughts about how I'd stroke her and shield her from Mrs. Pridham and be like a human barrier, refusing to let anyone get near her, so no one could frighten her away. But then I turned the corner and stopped in complete amazement.

Silver was too occupied even to look up. Or maybe she recognized my tread and knew she was safe. She was licking a little slimy ball with a thin black and white coat, and I realized that this kitten had only just been born. Then my eyes widened as I saw that there was another little kitten nestling in the crumpled, messy pile of dust sheets. It had slightly more fur than the one that had just been born, and its tiny face was utterly beautiful. Its eyes were closed and it seemed so peaceful and serene.

"Oh Silver! You clever girl!" I whispered in my

gentlest voice, as I crouched down. "You clever, clever girl!"

Then from behind me came loud footsteps and I turned to see Mrs. Pridham striding over.

"Ssh!" I told her strictly, as though I was the housemistress and she was the disobedient student. I softened my voice even though I really wanted to yell at her. "She's having kittens!"

I don't think I've ever seen such confusion on someone's face as that confusion I saw on Mrs. Pridham's just then. All the colour seemed to drain from her face and her hand shot out behind her in a signal to Mr. Monk to come no further. Then, as she took off her shoes and tiptoed barefoot across the loft, gliding and serious, I caught a glimpse of the others hovering behind Mr. Monk. They hadn't gone back to the dorm after all.

"See," I whispered when Mrs. Pridham was right beside me. "See what a clever cat she is?"

Mrs. Pridham kneeled down, her face still pale, her eyes on the newborn kitten, who had somehow found where to suckle.

"Good girl, Silver," I murmured. "Good girl."

"Good girl, Silver," came Mrs. Pridham's gentle voice beside me. And in that moment, the words of Hannah's text came back to me...

Mrs. P def not animal person but v symp so shd b ok.

How right those words had turned out to be. It had taken an outsider to point out something none of us had fully realized: Mrs. P *was* sympathetic.

But would it be okay? Or put another way, *would Mrs. Pridham let Silver stay?*

Come to think of it, would she let *me* stay?

Chapter Nine

"**A**mazing!" said Sasha in a hushed whisper.

A fifth kitten had just been born, and Silver had an audience of seven people all encouraging her with gentle words. Earlier on Emily hadn't been happy about the audience. She'd suggested I should be the only one to stay with Silver, but, while Mr. Monk tiptoed off, the others simply couldn't tear themselves away. Even Mrs. Pridham. And we'd all watched the third kitten being born, keeping the deepest silence out of respect for Silver, but mainly out of sheer wonder at what we were lucky enough to be witnessing. The kitten had been dripping wet and very slimy around its mouth and Silver had spent ages cleaning it up until it looked as lovely as the other two. Then, just like those other two, the third one had started to suckle its mother.

When Emily had explained that we might have to wait another half-hour or even an hour for the next one to be born, the others had crept away, and so had Mrs. Pridham, leaving just Emily and me. We'd looked at each other wide-eyed and filled with two sorts of wonder – the wonder of nature and a fearful wondering about what the future held for Silver.

"How do you know if there are more kittens to come?" I'd asked.

"I can just tell from the shape of her," Emily had answered. "I've seen farm cats having kittens."

And now it was about an hour and half later and Mrs. Pridham and the others were back, watching the fifth kitten suckling its mother. This one was beautiful.

"Look! It's totally black," said Izzy. "That means it's lucky!"

"Isn't it sweet, Mrs. Pridham?" said Antonia, beaming like mad.

Mrs. Pridham nodded. When she didn't speak I glanced sideways at her, but I couldn't read her expression. Maybe she was thinking about the punishment she was going to give me as soon as she'd dealt with Silver and her family.

"The black one's my favourite!" said Nicole. "Why don't we call him Lucky?"

Then the others each said which was their favourite, all choosing a different one. Except Emily, who was quietly concentrating on the birth.

"What about you, Bry?" Sasha asked me. "Which is your favourite kitten?"

"I...don't really have one," I answered, as I watched Silver's limp body being prodded and pushed by her little kittens, who had nearly all scrambled their way to a teat now and were sucking away. It was true, I didn't have a favourite. Well, apart from Silver herself. She meant so much to me. I would do anything I could to help her.

Sasha turned to Emily. "I wish I could hold one, but I suppose they're too young, aren't they?"

But Emily was watching Silver intently. "She's about to have another one," she said, ignoring Sasha's question.

"How can you tell?" asked Nicole.

"See how she's kind of shuddering? She's having contractions."

"She must be exhausted," murmured Mrs. Pridham.

Emily was frowning.

"Is she okay, Ems?" I asked, starting to feel prickles of concern.

Emily didn't reply, and we all stayed silent for a good five minutes until a sixth kitten slid out of Silver and lay quite still. It was absolutely minute, and didn't resemble a kitten at all, but for its little tufts of grey fur sprouting out from wrinkled red skin. So ugly. Definitely my favourite kitten.

From behind me I heard a gasp. I think it was Sasha.

"Oh dear..." murmured Mrs. Pridham, and I swallowed, turning sharply to look at Emily to see why she thought this kitten was so still.

Silver got up suddenly, her kittens tumbling and rolling off her. They stumbled on their weak little legs and fell over again while their mother only seemed to care about the still little kitten that lay on the very edge of the dust sheet. She began to lick it, giving it all her attention, until slowly, slowly it started to move. Then it let out a high-pitched mew and Silver flopped down again. A moment later the kitten latched on to one of her teats, and before long it was sucking away just like the others. Its mother looked exhausted, and though the kittens all latched on happily, Silver was shuffling around. She seemed uncomfortable.

"Are there any more to come, Ems?" asked Izzy.

Emily shook her head. "No, I don't think so."

"Thank goodness for that!" said Mrs. Pridham.

There was a short, awkward silence. It was as though the show was over and now I had to face the music. Mrs. Pridham stood up, which seemed to make the awkwardness spread to the others.

"Well—" she began. But she got no further.

"I think Silver needs a vet," came Emily's voice, serious and strained.

Mrs. Pridham crouched down again. "A vet?"

"Why? What's the matter?" I asked, feeling an urgency to know it was nothing serious, but fearing Emily's answer.

"Something's not right. She's in pain. She's trying to get the kittens off her," said Emily. "I mean, I can only say what I've seen on the farm, but if a cow was looking like that, Dad would call the vet for sure."

I felt a tightness in my throat as I looked at Mrs. Pridham.

"I'll go down and phone a vet now," she said after frowning at the floor for a moment.

"Oh, thank you," I said, with a rush of gratitude. "Th-thank you."

* * *

About an hour later the vet still hadn't arrived. Emily and I were the only two people with Silver. The others were all at supper but we weren't hungry and Mrs. Pridham had said we could stay.

"Only till the vet arrives," she'd warned us. Then she'd given another instruction. "Now, I'm saying to you what I've said to the others. Even if everything turns out well, there's no question that we can keep the cat or the kittens. We don't have the facility and it's not appropriate. We break up for the summer holidays in under two weeks and Mr. Pridham and I have got a holiday booked shortly afterwards. We're away for a month, and as it's too early to separate the kittens from their mother there's no choice but to find a home for the whole family." My eyes had been fixed on Silver as Mrs. Pridham had been talking, and my heart felt heavy seeing the way she kept pushing the kittens away. It could only mean she was in pain. "I'll ask the vet's advice when he arrives," Mrs. Pridham carried on quietly. "And we'll take it from there."

My whole body had felt limp and lifeless the more Mrs. Pridham had talked. And I'd started to make a plan to call Anna to see if we could have Silver and her kittens at home. Our house is quite big and so is our garden, but even if Anna said we had to give the kittens away to good homes, it would be all right as long as she agreed to keep Silver. That was all I wanted.

I was desperate to stroke Silver but Emily thought we should leave her alone and just sit with her. I couldn't bear the way she kept looking at me. She seemed to be saying, "*Do* something!" And I just kept murmuring to her that the vet was on his way, even though she didn't have a clue what I was on about. Emily put her arm round my stiff shoulders once or twice. "The vet will sort her out, Bry, don't worry," she said. But somehow, the anxious look on her face didn't match her words, and I was worried sick about what might be the matter with poor Silver.

"Listen, someone's coming. I can hear a man's voice," Emily said suddenly.

I got up and went over to the stairs. The man had a brown case. He smiled up at me and said hello in a kindly voice. "I'm Duncan."

"I'm…Bryony, and this is Emily."

Emily scarcely turned round, but she started talking immediately and I wondered whether this was how her dad talked when they called the vet out on their farm. "The cat's name is Silver and she's had six kittens over the last few hours. The last one looked as though it might not survive but it seems fine now. Silver struggled to give birth to that one, though, and she doesn't seem to want her kittens suckling her."

"Dear me," murmured Duncan, laying his case down behind him so as not to frighten Silver, and reaching out his hand to her to let her sniff it. "There we are," he said in a sing-song voice. "Let's take a look, shall we?"

The kittens had been making their high squeaky mewing sounds off and on for the last hour but now they were making a constant noise.

"I think we should leave Duncan to examine... Silver, girls," came Mrs. Pridham's voice from behind us. "And you two need to get some supper before prep."

Supper? Prep? How could normal life go on when Silver had just had six kittens but she wasn't well enough to feed them? "I'd rather stay here," I said, trying to keep my voice calm.

"No, come on, Bry," said Emily. "Silver's not going anywhere. Duncan will look after her."

"I'll take some blood and get it analysed," he said. "It's probably a uterus infection... Then we'll see what we can do."

"There you are," said Emily. "She'll be fine. Come on, Bry."

I knew it made sense. I'd be starving hungry later if I didn't eat now.

"She'll need food and water to keep her strength up," Duncan was saying to Mrs. Pridham as Emily and I left.

My body felt stiff and strange from being still for so long, and my legs trembled a bit as I followed Emily down the stairs.

"A cat and six kittens! That's amazing!"

The whole school seemed to be buzzing with the news of what had happened in the Forest Ash attic. There was hardly anyone left in the dining hall because Emily and I were so late getting to supper, but on the way over we'd passed loads of people who'd asked about Silver and that's how we knew that word had spread. Before we'd even left Forest Ash we'd met the Year Nines from the dorm near the cleaning room and they'd pretended to be cross with us.

"Yeah, cheers for telling us, you two!" said Nadia.

"Don't worry about us! We've only been having nightmares for the last week!" That was Annie.

"Sorry. But we thought Mrs. P would go mad..." I said, trying to explain.

"But she seems okay about it, doesn't she?" said Gemma. "At least she sounded okay with us... I mean, not cross or anything."

"She was cross earlier on," Emily told them.

"And she's not letting us keep Silver *or* her kittens," I added, sounding angrier than I'd intended.

The three Year Nines had gone quiet after that, and looked at me as though I was completely mad.

And now Emily and I were sitting in the dining hall, talking about them as we ate our salads.

"It was just the way they looked at us," I said.

"Yes, like we were out of our trees, or something."

"They obviously assumed Mrs. P would never agree to keep Silver and the kittens in a million years."

"The thing is, Bry," said Emily carefully, as though she didn't want to upset me, "it's probably no wonder she isn't letting us keep them, is it?"

I didn't answer but I felt sad, because in my heart of hearts I knew that Emily was right. I'd thought it through myself. We couldn't keep them in the attic. Kittens soon became cats. In the winter it would be freezing with the window open, and they'd all start going downstairs into the cleaning room looking for a way out. Then they'd nip into the corridor whenever anyone opened the door. And in no time at all they'd be roaming all over Forest Ash. No, I knew the only answer was to let a nice animal-loving family take them all. But then my mind came straight back to Anna and Dad and I decided to call them then and there. Maybe...just maybe...

"And don't forget to text Hannah too," Emily reminded me when I told her what I was going to do. So I quickly did that first.

Hi Han, Silver has 6 fab kittens! My thumbs hovered over my phone as I racked my brain for what else to say. Should I mention that the vet was with Silver right now? Should I say that it looked pretty unlikely that we'd be able to keep Silver, let alone the kittens? In the end I just put *Luv Bry*. I'd leave it another day before telling Hannah any bad news, and let her enjoy the good news first. Maybe Silver would make a swift recovery and she and the kittens would go to a lovely family who lived really nearby and Silver would still come here to visit. That would be a nice thing to be able to report to Hannah.

I called home but it went to voicemail so I left a message for Anna or Dad to get back to me. I didn't want to start talking to the answerphone about how I thought it would be a good idea if we adopted a cat and six kittens. It might not go down too well. No,

I had to explain it carefully, and make them realize how desperate I was.

Emily and I got back from supper to be told that everything was under control and that the vet had taken a blood sample from Silver, which was being analysed. Mrs. Pridham also said she'd managed to get hold of a double feeding bowl from our Head of school, Ms. Carmichael, whose cat had died of old age about a year earlier.

After that it was impossible to concentrate during prep, mainly because of worrying about Silver. But there was another huge worry lurking in the back of my mind too. I was doing my best to ignore it, thrusting it back every time it tried to creep forwards. But I couldn't forget that Mrs. Pridham hadn't even given me a proper telling-off, let alone a punishment after all the wrong things I'd done. I ran through the list, my heart hammering against my ribs. Had I really ignored her when she'd told me to go to the dorm, then shushed her when she'd appeared behind me in the loft? I wondered if anyone else at Silver Spires had ever behaved so appallingly. I swallowed as I imagined her telling me I'd been expelled.

I'd worked out that the reason she hadn't said anything yet was because she was waiting to get the kittens sorted out before she started sorting *me* out, and I could feel an embarrassed awkwardness hanging between us after prep when I went to ask her if I could go up and see Silver.

I was relieved when she gave me permission to see Silver before I got ready for bed, but I knew she was just hanging on, biding her time, waiting for the moment when she was going to sit me down and tell me what punishment she'd decided on. I felt a tight knot in my stomach at the thought.

One or two people asked why *I* was allowed to see Silver, when no one else was.

"Because it's all down to Bryony that Silver had her kittens at Forest Ash, that's why!" Emily replied, flinging her sharpest stare at anyone who dared to come back at her.

But nobody did. In fact I felt quite touched at the way people seemed to be rooting for me. Already there were murmurs that we ought to be allowed to keep the kittens. It made me sad that no one seemed too bothered about Silver, though. They just thought it would be sweet to have kittens running around.

In the end Emily came up with me too. She looked as shocked as I felt at the sight of Silver. The poor cat seemed so miserable and weak and every so often a dreadful noise came out of her. It was like no sound I'd ever heard before. The kittens were still mewing and scrambling to get to her teats but they didn't stay still for long and I was so worried that they might not be getting enough milk.

"Has Duncan phoned with the blood sample results?" I asked Mrs. Pridham, when I'd left Silver, with a lump in my throat.

"Yes, just this minute. It's…exactly as he thought – an infection of the uterus. He's going to drop off the antibiotics and a few sachets of soft food for her. I'll crush the first tablet into the food for her to take tonight. Then…as soon as she's better in…a day or two, we'll start to take steps to have them all moved. Duncan thinks he knows someone who'll take the whole family, so I might not need to advertise."

"What about a litter tray?" I asked, desperately trying to get away from talk of Silver leaving Forest Ash, and get back to the arrangements for right now.

"Ms. Carmichael has given us hers and Duncan brought a bag of cat litter. I asked him whether she ought to be taken into his surgery but he said it was safer not to disturb her."

I nodded, feeling exhausted.

Then Emily spoke and I suddenly realized she hadn't said a single word until now. "Mrs. Pridham...?"

"Yes?"

"N-nothing. It's all right."

"Right, well let's leave it there for now. Off you go to bed."

The moment we were alone again, walking up to our dorm, I asked Emily what she'd been about to say.

"Nothing. Well...nothing much."

I know my best friend and I could tell she was keeping something from me. And the only reason she might be keeping something from me was because she thought it would alarm me. I didn't press her right then. Instead I looked at my phone to see if there were any messages, and found a text from Anna. *At work. Special dinner. Will call first thing 2moro. Hope all good wi you. Love you. A x*

Then I followed Emily into the dorm and climbed up onto my bed. I looked down at her. "Truth talk," I said in a no-nonsense voice.

She sighed a massive sigh, then slowly came towards my bed, as though a truth talk was the very last thing she wanted to have at that moment. The others came to join us, exchanging darting glances, wondering what was going on. I didn't waste a second, just asked Emily what she'd been going to say to Mrs. Pridham.

"Truthfully," I reminded her, firmly.

She sighed. "It's probably nothing, but I don't think you're supposed to give antibiotics to cats that are suckling kittens."

There was a pause while I tried to work out why on earth Duncan had decided to give them to Silver then.

"We had a cow that had to have its calf taken away from it to be hand reared," Emily went on, "because the cow would have died without antibiotics." The moment the words were out of her mouth she looked as though she'd given herself a horrible shock and was scrambling to get out of it. "I don't mean that Silver's going to die. I mean, Duncan obviously knows what he's doing and everything. Mrs. P might have got it wrong, maybe they're not antibiotics, maybe they're just some kind of tablets to relieve the pain..." She trailed off, her cheeks turning bright pink. "You shouldn't have made me have a truth talk, Bry."

She was right, I shouldn't.

Because now I was worried sick about Silver.

Chapter Ten

That night I hardly slept at all, and neither did Emily. We kept on whispering in the dark, asking each other if we could hear anything. There were no sounds of kittens mewing, which filled me with a new dread, and every so often we heard an awful strangled cry from Silver. I found it unbearable to think of her in such pain, with nothing and no one to help her.

In the morning Emily and I went straight to Mrs. Pridham to ask her if we could see Silver and the kittens. We wanted to find out if she'd eaten her tablet the night before and to ask when Duncan was coming back too. She said he should be arriving any time and Emily and I begged to be let off breakfast. Mrs. Pridham hesitated, then agreed to allow it this once, as long as our friends brought us back some fruit. Her face seemed to be set hard when she looked at me and I feared the punishment I was due, but I kept on pushing it to the back of my mind so I could concentrate on Silver.

As soon as Duncan arrived we asked him if we could go up to see Silver with him, and he said that would be all right.

She looked so frail and thin, her chest rising and falling much too quickly as she breathed hard. Three of the kittens were suckling and she didn't seem to have the energy to stop them, even if she'd wanted to. The other three were rolling about nearby. At least the kittens seemed all right, but Silver... I swallowed.

"Is she going to be all right?" I asked Duncan, dreading the answer.

"Well, the next twelve hours are critical." He paused, then turned a very grave expression on us. "I ought to warn you that it's not looking good, I'm afraid. You see, the problem was finding antibiotics that she could take safely while suckling her young."

Emily and I exchanged a glance. She'd been right then.

"The ones I've given her might not prove to be as effective as some others could have been, but at least they won't affect the kittens."

I looked at my watch and suddenly needed to know exactly what Duncan was saying. "Twelve hours? So if she's still...okay at quarter past eight tonight, she'll definitely be...all right for ever."

Duncan looked at his own watch and paused before answering. I couldn't tell if he was calculating the time or wondering whether I could cope with the truth. "Yes, I'd say so... Yes."

Emily squeezed my hand and I realized Mrs. Pridham was right behind us. I hadn't even heard her footsteps on the stairs. "You'd better come down now, girls. You can pop over again at lunchtime."

It worried me now that Mrs. Pridham was being so kind and still hadn't punished me. It made me think she knew Silver wasn't going to survive and she was letting me see her alive for the last time. The morning passed more slowly than any other morning I could remember. Or so it felt. Emily and I bolted down the smallest amount of lunch, then rushed back to Forest Ash.

We knocked on Mrs. Pridham's door and as we waited I glanced sideways and noticed how pale Emily's face was beneath her freckles.

"I've been up there twice," Mrs. Pridham told us quietly, as she followed us upstairs. "She's had her second tablet but it's not...looking good, I'm afraid."

Those were the same words that Duncan had used. I didn't like them and didn't ever want to hear them again.

Walking across the attic floor was awful. Emily was holding my hand and I was gripping hers tightly, dreading what I was going to find around the corner. At first, when I saw Silver, I feared the worst had happened and felt my throat tighten. Wondering how her kittens could survive without her, I crouched down and stroked her head lightly, and her eyes opened just enough to blink at me very slowly.

"Don't die," I whispered, feeling my tears gathering, but blinking them away, because I never cry. "Please don't die."

"Only seven hours and ten minutes to go till the danger's over," said Emily with a catch in her voice.

Mrs. Pridham patted my shoulder. "The kittens

are doing wonderfully well, aren't they?"

I know she was only trying to cheer us up but it made me cross that she didn't seem to care about Silver.

I turned to Emily. "What'll happen to the kittens if…she doesn't make it?"

"I think they'll have to be bottle fed," said Emily.

Then Mrs. Pridham's phone rang and she moved right away from us and spoke softly.

"That was Duncan," she said, coming back a moment later to find us in exactly the same positions, taking turns to give Silver the gentlest of strokes. "He's coming round later to see how she is, but in the meantime we should try to help her drink some water."

I was wondering how we could possibly do that when the water bowl was right next to Silver but she was just ignoring it. She'd hardly touched her food either, and Mrs. Pridham said she'd had to push the tablet into her mouth. She wasn't even certain that Silver had swallowed it. Emily said she thought she must have done, then she dipped her finger in the bowl and put it right next to Silver's mouth. After a moment, Silver licked off the tiny drop of water. We took turns offering our wet fingers after that, but even so she was only getting a tiny amount of water. Still, it must have been better than nothing.

"The lady that Duncan mentioned..." Mrs. Pridham began suddenly. "Well, it turns out that it's not convenient for her to have the kittens after all."

"So why can't *we* keep them?" The words were out of my mouth before I could stop them.

"No...I've told you, that's out of the question." Mrs. Pridham had spoken very firmly, and I knew there was no point in pleading with her. I'd noticed she'd not mentioned Silver, just said that the lady couldn't have the kittens. And somehow I didn't think that was because the lady was quite happy to have Silver but not the kittens. No, it was because Mrs. Pridham didn't think Silver was going to live. My hand shook as I dipped my fingertip into the water bowl.

Emily and I came down from the attic feeling drained. She put her arm round me as we walked along the corridor, then we told the others the awful news in the dorm as they stood silently looking at us with big questioning eyes.

"The kittens are going to be okay but we're not sure about Silver," I said immediately, because I suddenly couldn't bear their grave faces for a second longer. I could feel tears springing to my eyes but I looked down and blinked hard to make them go away.

Then Mrs. Pridham knocked and I noticed, as she opened the door, that there were quite a few girls hovering around on the landing just behind her. Mrs. Pridham explained to everyone that there was nothing we could do, and that the vet would be back in a little while to give Silver her next tablet.

"What's going to happen to the kittens?" asked Nicole.

I swallowed. Everyone was assuming Silver wouldn't survive. Emily's arm tightened round my shoulder.

All eyes were on Mrs. Pridham.

"We've not decided yet," she said firmly.

"But why exactly can't we keep them?" Nadia asked, pushing herself forward a bit so she was standing next to Mrs. Pridham.

"It's just not practical," came the answer. "I know they're sweet little kittens now, but they're going to grow into cats and a boarding house isn't the place for a lot of cats."

Then the bell went and Mrs. Pridham told us all

to go off to afternoon lessons. "Try not to worry, you two. The vet will do all he can."

As my eyes met Emily's, I realized it was true we were both worrying like mad. But my worry was for Silver, and Emily's was for me.

Afternoon school was even harder to get through than the morning had been. I'd switched my phone on in between lessons and found a text from Hannah and a message from Anna. Hannah's text read: *Whats happenin wi Silver and kitts?* Anna's voicemail was bright and breezy, saying she'd try again later, as I wasn't picking up. And I realized I hadn't even switched my phone on when I'd collected it from Matron that morning, I'd been so preoccupied with thoughts about Silver. I switched it off again immediately because I didn't feel like answering Hannah's question. It would only make her as sad as I was. Well...nearly. And I didn't feel like talking to Anna either. Or anyone really.

Mrs. Pridham met us as soon as we went in to Forest Ash. Even in the seconds before she spoke I was studying her face for signs of how Silver was, and I dared to allow myself the teeniest shred of hope – because her eyes were smiling.

"It's good news... Duncan thinks she's going to be all right!"

I closed my eyes with relief.

I was still brimming with happiness and hope as we set off to the attic to see Silver, but I stopped in my tracks when Mrs. Pridham said, "Ms. Carmichael's coming over shortly, girls. She feels, like I do, that we must make arrangements for the cat and her kittens to go to a proper home, as soon as possible."

I drew in my breath slowly and let it out again with a sigh. Something told me that we were getting nearer to the time when I'd be given my punishment. Why did Ms. Carmichael need to pay a personal visit to see the kittens? No, she wanted to see me and Emily. That's why she was coming. But nothing was Emily's fault and I would make sure I explained that straight away. I was the one who was responsible for encouraging Silver to stay in the loft.

When Emily and I got to the attic, Silver was lying on her back suckling all six kittens at the same time. She looked exhausted, but you could tell she wasn't struggling any more. She was still and serene, and at the sight of us she did a massive yawn, which made us both laugh.

"Oh, Silver, you really are much better!" I said, stroking her and putting my face close to hers. I felt her wet nose rubbing on my cheek and wondered if that was a cat kiss. But then I felt sad again, because I'd only just had the lovely surprise of finding Silver better and now I had to get used to the idea of her leaving Silver Spires.

"Maybe they won't be able to find anyone to take them," said Emily, reading my mind. "Then they'll *have* to stay here."

"But we break up in under two weeks," I reminded her. "And Mrs. Pridham said she was going away, didn't she?"

"Did your stepmum get back to you?" asked Emily.

"I'd forgotten about that. I'll ring her now."

Anna picked up immediately and was in her usual cheerful mood. I tried to spin the story out, making it as dramatic as possible and laying it on thickly about how Silver had nearly died. It was when I began to describe how adorable the kittens were that she said, "Sorry, Bryony, if you're building up to asking me if we can have Silver and the kittens at home, then I'd better stop you right there. I'm afraid the answer is no. Dad seems to have developed some kind of an allergic reaction to Fellini – you know, watery eyes and shortage of breath. So there's no way he'd ever think about taking on *one* cat of our own, let alone seven! I'm sorry."

I'd known they'd never let me adopt Silver and the kittens really, but I still felt awful as I disconnected because that was my last tiny ray of hope gone.

"Like we said before, we'll just have to hope it's someone near to Silver Spires who takes them on," said Emily. She'd obviously guessed from my side of the conversation that the answer was a definite no.

I didn't answer. My spirits were too low for talking.

"Look at the little tiny one," Emily went on. I could tell she was trying to cheer me up. "Its fur isn't so patchy now, is it?"

I told Emily something I'd been keeping to myself then. "In my head I call him Silver too, because he's the one who looks most like his mum and because if she'd died..." I could feel my voice shaking. "...I wanted there to be something kind of...left of her."

"But now you can think of another name for him!" said Emily, and I felt sorry for her that she was having to work so hard at trying to cheer me up. "He looks the exact colour of old ash that you see in a fireplace, doesn't he?" she went on. "Not quite as silver as his mum, more greyish."

"Ash," I repeated thoughtfully. "Yes."

Then we looked at each other and grinned. "Forest Ash!" said Emily with a note of triumph in her voice. "That makes sense. Only…Ash for short!"

And that's when we heard two voices and two sets of footsteps coming upstairs. Emily's eyes widened. "Ms. Carmichael!" she mouthed.

"Ah, so this is where it's been happening," came Ms. Carmichael's calm, deep voice.

"Uh-huh," said Mrs. Pridham.

I gulped as I looked round, hearing this new, unfamiliar set of footsteps, surprisingly quiet, approaching our precious corner of the loft.

"Hello, girls," said Ms. Carmichael. But she scarcely gave us a glance. Her eyes were on Silver and the kittens. They were still nudging Silver for milk while she tried to clean herself. Ms. Carmichael broke into a smile as she bent down and tickled the side of Silver's face. I was glad that she did that before she said anything about the kittens. Mrs. Pridham was staring in surprise. "Oh my goodness, she's made an improvement even in the last hour!"

"Six of them!" said Ms. Carmichael. "What a job!" Then she reached towards the black one that was lying down quietly and very gently stroked the top of his head. "You're a calm little chap, aren't you?" she said. "Or chap-ess!" she added with a chuckle.

"He's called Lucky," said Emily.

"Lucky, eh?" Ms. Carmichael looked at us and asked which one we liked best.

It felt so odd having this conversation with the Head of school. I couldn't relax. My insides were completely knotted and my body was stiff and tense, still waiting for my telling-off. "That one..." I said carefully, pointing to Ash, who was curled up by Silver's tail.

"Ah! And what have you called it?"

"Ash," I answered quietly.

Ms. Carmichael reached out for him and very gently put him in my hands. "There you are. I think that's a very appropriate name!"

Emily did the smallest of gasps and I quickly looked at her. "I thought Silver might object," she explained, "but actually, she seems okay about it."

Ash was making little mewing sounds and wriggling like mad, but once he'd got used to the feel of my hands he was completely still so I snuggled him into my neck and felt his wet nose on my skin, just as I had with Silver. Then, all of a sudden, I felt like bursting into tears, because I wasn't going to see him or Silver again after we broke up for the holidays.

"Don't you think that's appropriate, Mrs. Pridham?" Ms. Carmichael was saying.

"I certainly do," said Mrs. Pridham.

There was something in their voices that made me look from one to the other of them. Something jokey that was connecting them both. Emily must have noticed it too, because she was eyeing them almost suspiciously.

Ms. Carmichael stood up briskly and brushed herself down. "Right, that's settled then. Forest Ash naturally gets first choice and they have chosen Ash."

It was as though I was dreaming. Or maybe I'd gone mad. I didn't seem to be able to understand what Ms. Carmichael meant.

"You mean..." Emily began, turning to me with shining eyes.

"You mean..." I echoed faintly, not daring to believe my ears. Not yet.

Mrs. Pridham broke into a chuckle. "We thought you'd be pleased. I explained to Ms. Carmichael that you'd broken a lot of rules, but it was for the right reasons..."

"Yes, she was trying to protect Silver," said Emily, standing closer to me.

"Exactly," said Ms. Carmichael. "And I didn't

think we could have our students going to such lengths without making sure there was a happy outcome!"

"So each house will have a kitten. Like a kind of mascot," Mrs. Pridham finished off.

Except that it wasn't finished. No one had mentioned poor Silver.

"What about..."

"I thought I'd like to have this clever mum myself at home," said Ms. Carmichael, bending down again to give Silver a stroke. "I lost my old cat last year and I've missed having a companion about the place. I'll have to take all the kittens as well once we've broken up, because of course they can't be separated from their mum just yet."

My heart seemed suddenly too big for my body and my eyes were filling up with tears. "Thank you very much," I managed to say in a shaky voice as one or two tears spilled out and rolled down my cheeks.

Then more and more followed until I was properly crying. And Mrs. Pridham folded me into her and said, "There we are, there we are," and Emily held tight to my hand just like Dad had done when we were burying Lana. And that was when the clearest picture of Mum's face came into my mind and I realized I was crying for Mum and also for Lana, shedding all the tears that the five-year-old me hadn't shed, and the more I cried, the more I felt myself letting go of the past and coming back to the present, where the tears were not of sadness, but of happiness, because of what Ms. Carmichael had said.

Emily gave my hand one last squeeze, then let go of it and went to hug an amazed Ms. Carmichael, as only my best friend would dare to. "Thank you soooooooooo much!" she said dramatically. "For ever and ever, amen!" she added.

So then everything seemed to fall into place and I couldn't wait to text Hannah the good news. Now she could come to Silver Spires next term without worrying about the unknown, because Silver would be there and so would all her kittens.

"You know how the shamrock is the emblem of Ireland," Emily suddenly said, staring out of the window. "Well, Silver will be the emblem of Silver Spires, won't she?"

I nodded, because those words had slotted perfectly into my thoughts, like the last piece of a jigsaw puzzle.

"And all the new Year Sevens will feel a kind of special connection because they'll have their own cat in their boarding house," I added.

Ms. Carmichael nodded. "Exactly," she said.

Then Emily and I whizzed downstairs, along the landing and into Emerald, where the other four were waiting for us, their faces getting ready to hear the worst. So it was absolutely the best feeling ever telling them the best.

"Silver's better and Ms. Carmichael is going to take her, and each boarding house is going to have one of the kittens to keep for ever!" I gabbled, watching their faces break into massive smiles.

"Yay!" said Izzy, grabbing hold of Sasha's hands and spinning round with her.

"That's so brilliant!" said Nicole.

"*Fantastico!*" said Antonia. "*Meraviglioso!*"

"Good old Ms. Carmichael!" breathed Nicole.

"Good old Silver Spires," I added.

Emily hugged me tight, then pulled away suddenly and held up my hand like I'd just won a boxing match. "And good old Bryony Price!" she said in a big announcer's voice. "For sticking to her guns and solving the mystery of the Forest Ash ghost – and, more importantly, for turning it into a lovely future for Silver Spires." She dropped my hand suddenly and also dropped her voice back to normal. "Come on, let's go and spread the word round the whole school!"

"Yes! Come on!"

My friends plunged out of Emerald and spilled onto the landing, with me at the back. I was going slowly so I could reply to Hannah's text at the same time.

Silver and all kittens def staying at SS! Xx

I knew she'd be over the moon. And so was I.

I raced to catch up with the others and, when we were just outside the main building, looking up at the spires glinting in the sun, Emily suddenly stopped in her tracks. "I think it'll be easier if I just make one big announcement," she said. Then she flung out her arms and yelled out, "Silver's here for ever!"

And suddenly a window opened on the top floor of the main building and Katy popped her head out of it. I could see she had a few of her Year Eight friends with her, all peering out curiously.

"Silver Spires for ever!" called back one of them, who I think is called Georgie.

"She didn't say that!" we all heard Katy correcting Georgie and laughing. "She said 'Silver's here for ever!'"

"But that'll do fine!" I yelled up to them.

"Okay," said Georgie, grinning. "Three… two…one!"

Then the Year Eights from Hazeldean and us six Year Sevens from Forest Ash all called out together, "Silver Spires for ever!"

Bryony's Pet Quiz

It's so amazing having gorgeous Ash as our Forest Ash house pet! I always find it really comforting having a cat around. But what sort of pet suits you?

Q1. How would you describe yourself?
  a) Reliable and friendly
  b) Independent and sophisticated
  c) Calm and observant
  d) Sensitive and shy
  e) Affectionate and playful

Q2. What do you like to do in your spare time?
  a) Go for long walks or bike rides
  b) Go shopping or pamper yourself
  c) Chill out with a book
  d) Go swimming
  e) Snuggle up on the sofa to watch a film

Q3. If someone starts an argument with you, how are you most likely to react?
  a) Try to make friends again as quickly as possible
  b) Fight back

c) Refuse to get involved

d) Feel anxious and unsure what to do

e) Run away!

Q4. What would be your ideal holiday?

a) An activity break full of fun and excitement

b) A week or two lazing on the beach

c) An intrepid jungle exploration

d) Snorkelling over reefs in blue seas

e) Escaping to the countryside with friends

Answers:

Mostly As = a dog – so active and so much fun!

Mostly Bs = a cat – just like Silver!

Mostly Cs = a lizard – unusual but rewarding.

Mostly Ds = a fish – so relaxing to watch.

Mostly Es = a rabbit – great for cuddles!

Don't forget, there are lots of important things to consider when adopting a pet – it's a big commitment, so your whole family has to agree. But if they do, caring for a furry (or feathery or scaly) friend can be fantastic!

Bryony

Complete your
School Friends
collection!

First Term at Silver Spires   ISBN 9780746072240
Katy's nervous about going to boarding school for the first time – especially with the big secret she has to hide.

Drama at Silver Spires   ISBN 9780746072257
Georgie's desperate to get her favourite part in the school play, but she's up against some stiff competition.

Rivalry at Silver Spires   ISBN 9780746072264
Grace is eager to win in the swimming gala for Hazeldean – until someone starts sending mean messages about her.

Princess at Silver Spires   ISBN 9780746089576
Naomi hates being the centre of attention, but when she's asked to model for a charity fashion show, she can't say no.

Secrets at Silver Spires   ISBN 9780746089583
Jess is struggling with her schoolwork and has to have special classes, but she can't bear to tell her friends the truth.

Star of Silver Spires   ISBN 9780746089590
Mia longs to enter a song she's written in the Silver Spires Star contest, but she's far too scared to perform onstage.

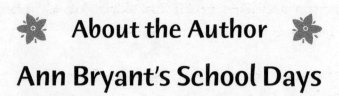

About the Author

Ann Bryant's School Days

Who was your favourite teacher?

At primary it was Mr. Perks – we called him Perksy.
I was in his class in Year Six, and most days he let
me work on a play I was writing! At secondary, my
fave teacher was Mrs. Rowe, simply because I loved
her subject (French) and she was so young and
pretty and slim and chic and it was great seeing
what new clothes she'd be wearing.

What were your best and worst lessons?

My brain doesn't process history, geography or
science and I hated cookery, so those were my least
favourite subjects. But I was good at English, music,
French and PE, so I loved those. I also enjoyed art,
although I was completely rubbish at it!

What was your school uniform like?

We had to wear a white shirt with a navy blue tie
and sweater, and a navy skirt, but there was actually
a wide variety of styles allowed – I was a very small

person and liked pencil-thin skirts. We all rolled them over and over at the waist!

Did you take part in after-school activities?
Well I loved just hanging out with my friends, but most of all I loved ballet and went to extra classes in Manchester after school.

Did you have any pets while you were at school?
My parents weren't animal lovers so we were only allowed a goldfish! But since I had my two daughters, we've had loads – two cats, two guinea pigs, two rabbits, two hamsters and two goldfish.

What was your most embarrassing moment?
When I was in Year Seven I had to play piano for assembly. It was April Fool's Day and the piano wouldn't work (it turned out that someone had put a book in the back). I couldn't bring myself to stand up and investigate because that would draw attention to me, so I sat there with my hands on the keys wishing to die, until the Deputy Head came and rescued me!

To find out more about Ann Bryant visit her website: www.annbryant.co.uk

Want to know more about the
Silver Spires girls?

Or try a quiz to discover which
School Friend you're most like?

You can even send Silver Spires e-cards
to your best friends and post your own
book reviews online!

It's all at

www.silverspiresschool.co.uk

 Check it out now!

For more fun and friendship-packed reads
go to **www.fiction.usborne.com**